Toddy

Also by Jane Peart

Orphan Train West for Young Adults
  Laurel
  Kit
  Ivy and Allison
  April and May

Edgecliffe Manor Mysteries
  Web of Deception
  Shadow of Fear
  A Perilous Bargain
  Thread of Suspicion

Jane Peart

Fleming H. Revell
A Division of Baker Book House Co
Grand Rapids, Michigan 49516

Published by Fleming H. Revell
a division of Baker Book House Company
P.O. Box 6287, Grand Rapids, MI 49516-6287

Adapted from *Homeward the Seeking Heart,* published in 1990

Printed in the United States of America

Library of Congress Cataloging-in Publication Data

Peart, Jane.
   Toddy / Jane Peart.
      p.   cm.
   "Adapted from Homeward the seeking heart"—T.p. verso.
   Summary: After her mother leaves six-year-old Toddy at the county children's home, she is chosen by a minister's wife to go West on the Orphan Train and is taken in by a wealthy widow as a companion for her sickly granddaughter.
   ISBN 0-8007-5716-5 (paper)
   [1. Orphans Fiction. 2. Christian life Fiction.] I. Peart, Jane. Homeward the seeking heart. II. Title.
PZ7.P32335To   2000
[Fic]—dc21   99-31962

For current information about all releases from Baker Book House, visit our web site:
                     http://www.bakerbooks.com

Rialto Theater, 1888

Music echoed down the drafty hall of the theater followed by thunderous applause. A moment later the dressing room burst open and two garishly costumed dancers entered. The blond plopped down into a straight chair in front of the spotted mirror and kicked off her red satin shoes.

"My feet are killin' me!"

"Shh, Mazel! You'll wake the kid!" A second dancer jerked one thumb toward a sleeping child stirring restlessly on a makeshift bed. The worn velvet cloak thrown across her like a blanket had slipped to the floor.

"Toddy? Oh, she's used to it. Ought to be by now. I been bringin' her to the theater almost every night for a long time."

"Nobody to leave her with?"

"Not without payin' a pretty penny."

"So, have you decided what you're goin' to do with her when we go on tour with this show, Mazel?"

Mazel opened a jar of makeup and began dabbing it on her face. "Not sure. I been thinkin' it over. This tour's the chance of a lifetime. I don't want to miss it. You heard what Barney said. We'll be playin' before the crowned heads of Europe!"

"If you can believe that," Flo replied doubtfully as she walked over to where the little girl lay sleeping.

She looked down at her, long lashes on rosy cheeks, the tangled red-gold curls spread on the tattered pillow. One small plump hand was tucked under her chin. The woman reached down to retrieve the velvet cloak and tuck it around the sleeping child.

"How old is she anyway?"

"Five goin' on six come June."

Flo straightened up and adjusted her costume's tarnished ruffles.

Mazel's voice dropped to a whisper. "I been thinkin' about sendin' word to her father. After all, she's his kid too. But I don't know where he is."

"We have to let Barney know by the end of the week. This here's the last night in Boston, and that tour starts just after the new year." Flo was looking at herself in the smeared mirror.

Sounds of high heels clattering on bare boards echoed down the drafty hallway. Loud music vibrated through the door of the shabby dressing room.

"There's always the county children's home." Mazel's raspy voice carried above the noise. "I could leave her there, and Johnny could come and get her."

Flo gasped. "You wouldn't!"

"Why not? Ain't that what we pay taxes for?"

"But she has parents—you and Johnny. That place is an orphanage! It's for kids who don't have any parents or kids who've been left on the street. Not there, Mazel."

"Got another idea?" Mazel snapped, tossing her brassy blond hair.

Flo didn't comment.

"After all, it'd only be temporary. I already made some inquiries. They'll take a kid like this if it's a case of necessity."

The loud music died down, and Flo lowered her voice. "But, Mazel, what do you know about the place? Have you gone there? Don't you think it's kinda risky?"

"What's risky about it? A roof over her head, three squares a day, a bed to sleep in, and other kids to play with. Sounds like heaven to me." Mazel faced the mirror and jammed a powder puff into its container.

"What if Johnny don't come and get her? Would they put her up for adoption?" Flo looked down at the little girl, slumbering peacefully and unaware that her fate was being decided.

"Of course not. You sign papers and that sort of thing. It's all legal. It'd be temporary."

Flo raised her eyebrows. "Maybe Barney would let you take her."

Mazel spun around and faced her. "I don't want to take her, Flo. Don't you get it? This is the chance I've been waitin' for all my life. I mean to take advantage of it, and I can't do that with a kid hangin' around my neck."

"Well, excuse me!" The words flung out as if they had been tight rubber bands wrapped around her tongue. "It ain't right, Mazel. Dumpin' your kid off in some orphanage. I couldn't do it if she was mine!"

"Well, she ain't yours, so mind your own business!"

End of discussion. Flo knew Mazel well. She rarely took advice. She usually did whatever suited her best.

A few days later, Mazel woke Toddy up and hurried her through a scanty breakfast of bread, jam, and tea.

"Sit up straight and stop wigglin'," Mazel ordered as she dragged the brush through Toddy's mass of curls.

Toddy held on to the sides of the chair on which she sat and tried not to squirm, squeezing her eyes shut tightly when the brush caught in a tangle. She realized that today her mother was in no mood to be patient.

"Now get dressed."

Toddy started but not quickly enough for Mazel.

"Here," she said, jerking Toddy's arms into the sleeves of her jacket. Shoving Toddy's tiny feet into her shoes, Mazel struggled with the buttonhook to fasten them, then jammed on Toddy's bonnet and tied the strings. As usual, this November morning in Boston was chilly.

"Here, take this," she said, handing Toddy her small valise.

Toddy was used to theater life. She had been carried into her first dressing room when she was less than two weeks old. Her lullabies had been the brassy sound of a vaudeville band. Old playbills and theater posters had been her first books and pictures. The backstage of a theater was like other children's cozy nurseries to her. Being left alone and moving from place to place did not bother her.

What did bother her was what had happened between her mother and Flo.

Normally, each night after the theater, Flo walked the deserted midnight streets back to the nearby boardinghouse with Toddy and her mother. The two women would laugh and chat while Toddy tagged along. But ever since that night they'd had the bad argument, Flo hadn't come along.

Toddy knew it had something to do with her. Having grown up among adults, the little girl had learned early in life to make herself scarce during grown-up conversations. She had heard part of the conversation that night. They had been talking about her. But what was an orphanage? And why was Flo upset?

"Hurry up, Toddy, we ain't got all day." Mazel was standing by the apartment door. "I got to be at the train station by ten-thirty, and we have a long way to go before that."

The two of them got to the trolley stop just as the streetcar rounded the bend. They climbed the high step into the car, and Mazel bought two tickets. Then they found seats in the nearly empty car. Toddy enjoyed the rocking motion as the car sped along the tracks, the bell jangling merrily in the morning air. "Here's where you want to get off, lady!" the driver called out just as the car jerked to a sudden stop at the bottom of a steep hill.

Way up at the top stood a large, strange, stone building. Toddy looked at her mother curiously. She wondered what kind of new adventure awaited them this time.

After reaching the door, Mazel straightened her hat and adjusted her feather boa before ringing the doorbell. She leaned over toward Toddy and retied the child's bonnet strings, "You're goin' to like it here, Toddy, you'll see."

A few minutes later, they were standing in a long room with a high ceiling. A woman with a frown on her face and little half glasses that cut across her large nose sat behind a huge desk at one end.

To Toddy's surprise, her mother suddenly began to weep into her handkerchief.

"I have no one to turn to, Miss Clinock," she said between sniffles. "There's nothing I want more than to be able to make a home for my little girl. But I can't do that now. With the money I'll be paid on this tour, when I come back I'll—" she stopped and blew her nose.

"Yes, Mrs. Todd," Miss Clinock interrupted, the creases between her dark brows growing deeper. "But just so you'll fully understand—" She passed Mazel a sheaf of papers. "Please read these carefully before you sign them."

The only sounds Toddy could hear were the loud ticking of the wall clock, the rustle of mysterious papers turning as Mazel skimmed them, and the tapping of Miss Clinock's pen on the surface of the wooden desk. After a few minutes, her mother picked up a nearby pen and signed one of the papers.

"This seems to be in order. Except—" Miss Clinock's eyes peered over her glasses, "you have no address for the father?"

"No, ma'am, there's been no word from him in years."

"All right, Mrs. Todd, you can say good-bye to your daughter now. Then we will see that she is taken up to her dormitory and settled in."

Mazel bent down and gave Toddy a slight hug. "Now, Toddy, you do as you're told and be a good girl. I'll bring you something nice back from Europe, maybe a big French doll with real hair. You'd like that, wouldn't you?"

Her mother had often left her in new places with strangers, but Toddy sensed this time was different. For a single moment they looked at each other. Then Mazel blinked and turned away, but not before Toddy saw something in her mother's eyes she had never seen before. Something she could not name but recognized: abandonment.

Greystone

Toddy sat on the edge of the narrow bed. Her feet swung back and forth in itchy black woolen stockings and sturdy black shoes laced to the ankles. She smoothed down the front of the blue muslin pinafore buttoned over the coarse cotton dress. Then she turned up the hem and examined the flannel petticoat and plain pantaloons she had been given to wear.

Toddy shrugged her shoulders. She liked the bright colors and patterns of the clothes her mother had a seamstress cut down for her better. She loved frilly lace and shiny ribbons. These clothes were so plain. But it didn't matter if she had to wear them. She wouldn't be here long anyway.

The young girl looked around the long room with its high windows and double row of small iron cots. Beside each bed was a chest of drawers with a white enamel washbowl and pitcher. Next to it was an unpainted wooden stool.

This was the "orphanage" Flo had talked about.

Because her mother had often left her with people she scarcely knew, Toddy was not afraid of this new place.

Strangers didn't bother her, and she enjoyed different surroundings.

As she sat there, Toddy heard the sound of running feet on the linoleum hall floor outside. The muffled sound of children's voices touched her ears. Then the dormitory doors burst open and in rushed a group of girls. They halted at the sight of the stranger.

A tall, chunky, redheaded girl pushed to the front. "Hey you! You're new, ain't you? I'm Molly B. What's your name?"

Toddy smiled and got to her feet. "I'm Toddy," she replied enthusiastically.

The girl walked forward followed by the rest of the troop. She shoved her fat freckled face right up to Toddy's. "Think you're smart, don't you?"

Toddy wasn't used to being around other children, but she recognized a bully when she met one. This girl with the squinty eyes was threatening her.

"No, I don't think I'm smart, but I can show you a trick!"

"What kind of trick?" The girl seemed startled by Toddy's response.

"Stand back," Toddy said pleasantly.

All eyes watched. Toddy moved out into the aisle, took a deep breath, and executed a series of cartwheels down the length of the room. Her life in the theater had taught her a thing or two. Over and over she went until she had finished the last one. Immediately, the delighted onlookers clustered around her.

Suddenly, everyone heard the loud snap of wooden clappers.

"Come girls, time for outdoor recreation!" The woman's deep voice had a commanding tone. Toddy soon learned this was the dormitory matron. "Get your sweaters and form a line to go out to the play yard."

Instantly, the girls lined up, and Toddy smiled. She had won this one. The girls had accepted her.

Over the next few months, Toddy received two post-cards from Mazel. One was a picture of Buckingham Palace in London, and the other had been written on a train to France. She kept the two cards under her pillow and took them out, rereading them until the edges were worn. After that, nothing else came. Before long, the seed of possibility that her mother might never come back began to take root in Toddy's little heart.

One day, Molly B. confronted her in the hall.

"Is your real name Zephronia Victorine Todd?" she demanded.

Toddy drew herself up and replied, "Yes it is. Why?"

"I'll tell you why, Miss Smarty. I saw your name on the list in Miss Clinock's office. You've been transferred from 'temporary' to 'permanent.' That means you're just like all the rest of us now. An *orphan*. No mother, no father, no home!"

With this, Molly B. stuck out her tongue and made an awful face. Then she laughed and ran off down the hall.

A cold chill like an icy finger trailed down Toddy's spine. Up until now, Toddy had held on to the hope Mazel would show up with the big French doll and they would go "home" together. From that moment on, Toddy buried that hope deep within her. On the outside, her smile and twinkling eyes kept her popular with the staff and other orphans. On the inside, however, she had been abandoned. She had no one.

One day, a new girl with neatly braided shiny brown hair arrived at Greystone. Her name was Kit Ternan. The teacher assigned her to share a double school desk with Toddy. The two little girls used the same reader and slate to do sums. When the recess bell rang, Toddy escorted Kit to the long tables where they picked up their mid-morning "tea" of a slice of buttered bread and a mug of watery cocoa.

Kit was the quietest person Toddy had ever known, but little by little, Toddy's warmth overcame Kit's shyness. When Kit was given the cot next to Toddy's in the dormitory, the two girls whispered long into the night. They became best friends.

A few months later, a third young girl named Laurel Vestal arrived at Greystone. She looked like the French doll Toddy had imagined her mother might have brought her from France. She had rosy cheeks, round brown eyes, and dark curls that tumbled over her shoulders and reached her waist in back.

The orphans watched the newcomer sitting on the little stool beside her cot, placed between Kit and Toddy. Dressed in a blue velour coat with a short scalloped cape and matching bonnet, she sat with her arms crossed. Her mouth was trembling. Tears hovered brightly in her dark eyes.

For three days, Laurel refused to change into the orphanage uniform. Toddy and Kit could hear her cry herself to sleep each night. On the third night, Toddy and Kit both crept out of their beds to sit on either side of her. One took Laurel's hand while the other gently stroked her hair away from her tear-stained face.

Eventually, Laurel did change her clothes. Dressed in the drab cotton dress, the new orphan entered the classroom for her first day of school. She took an empty desk near Toddy and Kit. At the recess bell, Toddy and Kit ran over to her, took her hands, and led her out to the recreation yard.

From then on, an unspoken bond was forged. The "Three Musketeers," as the staff came to call them, were developing a friendship that would last for the rest of their lives.

3

Meadowridge

The enormous Victorian house with its three tiers of balconies and peaked roof loomed on a hilltop over the town of Meadowridge. Mrs. Olivia Hale, back from church, went up the front steps to the porch and turned briefly to look back down on the town. Just beyond its pleasant houses and well-kept yards lay rolling pastures with grazing cattle, brightly painted barns, and a long winding river. After striking it rich in gold, her late husband, Ed, had chosen this spot because of this view.

Mrs. Hale opened the door and walked inside. A tall, handsome woman in her mid-fifties, she briefly stopped in front of the hall mirror to remove her Sunday hat and smooth her graying hair. She adjusted the black onyx brooch attached to the high collar of her black dress and moved into the nearby parlor.

Settled in a sculptured mahogany armchair by the bay window, Olivia thought about the morning's sermon. The face of the young visiting preacher had been earnest, his eyes searching the congregation as he spoke.

"I have spent two days in your beautiful town and the surrounding countryside. I've walked your shady streets and driven by your neat farmhouses along the hillsides.

And I've seen evidence of prosperity and contentment everywhere."

His words affected her now as they had just an hour before. Olivia glanced at the elaborate gold-framed portrait of Ed over the black-marble fireplace. Even after twenty years, she still missed the towering, raw-boned fellow with his thundering voice and glass-shattering laugh. Would *he* agree with this idea that had so unexpectedly rooted itself in the soil of her heart? What would he think?

The minister's words came back to her once more.

"Picture, if you will, two young boys, seven and eight years old, huddled in a deserted alley, their clothes ragged, their feet without shoes, freezing in the cold of the New England winter. Consider the plight of three pitiful youngsters hovering in a doorway, abandoned by their alcoholic father."

From her pew near the front, Olivia had been able to see the lines of concern etched across the pastor's young brow.

"You are so blessed here in Meadowridge. If you have any feelings of compassion, I plead with you now to consider what I am going to propose."

There in the parlor, Olivia's thoughts abruptly turned as her eyes caught the huge diamond solitaire she wore next to the thin gold band Ed had placed on her finger when, at sixteen, she had married him. She had been abundantly blessed in so many ways. Financially, Ed had struck it rich beyond their early dreams. Yes, she was blessed, and yet she had also lost so much in her lifetime. So much that she still wore the traditional black of someone in mourning.

First, of course, she had lost Ed. Her son, Richard, had been only ten when his father died. He had grown up with the legend of Big Ed and had spent his life trying to live up to his father's reputation.

It felt like it had happened just yesterday instead of seven years ago. Dick had been killed breaking in a new horse. The accident had happened right before the eyes of his fragile young wife, who had not lived long after that. Many said she had died of a broken heart. Olivia did not agree. No one dies of a broken heart. If so, *she* would already be dead too. Instead, Olivia had gone on living, bringing up her precious, delicate granddaughter, Helene.

She took in a long deep breath. She must consider this idea very carefully. The visiting minister's sermon this morning had touched a deep responding chord in her heart.

"In the past five years, the Rescuers and Providers' Society has been actively involved in rescuing these children and bringing them by train to families in the West." Matthew Scott's strong voice echoed across the silent congregation. "We plan to do this again this spring. My wife and I will be bringing a specified number of orphans ranging in age from five to ten by train, making stops at those towns where folks have agreed to take them into their homes and adopt them as their own."

As the pastor spoke, it was as if someone had nudged Olivia physically.

He continued. "I remember the shacks and tenements and bleak places I've visited back East in cities where dozens of children wait to be adopted. And I'm overwhelmed when I see the great contrast to life out here in Arkansas."

With that, the look in the man's eyes seemed to pierce into Olivia's soul.

"Because of this, I am encouraged today. Yes, I am bold today to ask you this question. You, who live in these bountiful circumstances," he moved his arms in a wide circle as he spoke, "will you take one of these unfortunate children into your home, to raise in a healthy Christian atmosphere?"

Olivia straightened up, tingling, alert. Should she consider such an amazing proposition? Should she dare to risk such a thing, not for herself, but for Helene?

"If any of you feel led to offer your home, my wife, Anna, and I will be here for the next few days. We'll be more than happy to answer all your questions.

"In closing, I remind you of Christ's own words: 'Whoever does this to the least of these, will have done it unto me.'

"Hundreds of families who've made this commitment have been blessed. If any of you can find it in your heart to do this, I guarantee that you'll be blessed too."

Olivia had never considered herself particularly spiritual. Oh, she was God-fearing and churchgoing, but she had always been a down-to-earth, sensible sort of person. That is why what happened to her was so startling. Unexpectedly she had felt the sting of tears. She felt as if the Lord himself were saying, "You have room in your house, Olivia. You have room in your heart too. Here is your answer: a companion for Helene."

In the quiet of the parlor, Olivia again looked at the man in the oil painting. Over the years, she often turned to this picture in times of indecision or anxiety. If only Ed were here. Her heart still mourned the loss of her husband and son. But the tragedy in her life had not stopped there. Not long after Dick's death, she had learned that her only granddaughter had a defective heart. Now, Olivia lived from day to day with the threat of losing her too.

Although Helene was nearly twelve, she had never been able to attend school or lead a normal child's life. Mrs. Hale could afford tutors and a nurse to care for her, but that was not enough. Helene was lonely for companionship, children her own age. The problem was that no normally active child was content to sit quietly and play lap games or do watercolors or read. And this was what Helene's frail health required.

The thought of adoption began to seem like a good idea. Yes, the Scotts could bring a suitable child to be her granddaughter's companion. Of course, she would have to outline the requirements—the personality, age, and interests. The idea now took a shape all its own. And, of course, it would have to be a girl.

Olivia rose, went to her desk, and took out her fine stationery with the swirled gold monogram at the top. She would invite Mr. Scott and his wife to tea while they were in Meadowridge. Meeting Helene would give them a better idea of what kind of child to place with her. She dipped her pen into the inkwell and began to write.

Boston

Anna Scott controlled a shudder as she and her husband approached the tall, forbidding stone building behind the black iron fence. The afternoon was gray, the sky heavy with dark clouds. A fierce wind was tossing the barren branches of the few trees. Even though it was the last week of March, there was not a sign of spring anywhere, not a crocus or green bud or even a robin. Boston was drab this time of year.

Anna took Matthew's arm with one hand as they mounted the stone steps. With the other, she held onto her bonnet while her cloak billowed behind her like a sail. As they waited for an answer to the doorbell, Anna gazed at her husband adoringly. This first year of their marriage, filled with its constant traveling and strange towns, had been a fulfilling one. Their love remained as steadfast as Matthew's determination to achieve his inspired vision.

Matthew's high-mindedness, lofty morals, and idealistic goals had drawn her to him ever since she had heard him speak at her church two years ago. His dream of taking every homeless child, abandoned or orphaned, to a Christian home in the rural heartland of the country was becoming Anna's dream as well.

Yet, she felt inadequate for the task. Anna had come from a sheltered home. What did she know about caring for a train carload of children traveling across the country? She had no real experience. She had been an only child, and her one attempt at teaching a Sunday school class had ended as quickly as it had started. She had no gift for keeping the lively eight- to ten-year-old youngsters in order.

How on earth would she manage this? Over and over, she found herself repeating a verse from Philippians. "I can do all things through Christ which strengtheneth me."

As she and her husband now waited at the door, she thought about this verse again. Just then Matthew turned and smiled as if he had been reading her thoughts. Anna smiled back. Somehow she would find a way. Today, on this dreary day in 1890, she and Matthew were fulfilling the call of God.

Greystone Orphanage was the last institution the couple was contacting to fill the quota of children they would be escorting out West.

"We have an appointment with Miss Clinock, your head matron," Matthew addressed the thin woman who opened the door. "Mr. and Mrs. Scott."

"She is expecting you. Please wait here. I'll tell her you've come." She disappeared down the dark hallway.

As they waited, they heard the tramp of dozens of little boots. Mrs. Scott turned her head in the direction of the sound. Two lines of little girls were descending the wide main staircase. At the bottom, the matron in charge herded them into a single line, straightening the line with pushes and shoves as she walked its length.

At first glance, the children all looked alike, dressed in identical buff cotton dresses, blue muslin pinafores, black stockings, and black high-top shoes. Then Anna's eyes were drawn to one particular child who returned her look. She had round blue eyes sparkling with mis-

22

chief, a turned-up nose, and dimples. Riotous red-gold curls had escaped the tight braids into which someone had attempted to confine her hair.

There was something appealing about the little girl. And the one just behind her, who had an enchanting beauty that even the drab institutional outfit could not hide. This girl was a cameo in miniature, with rosy porcelain cheeks, dark eyes, and wavy dark hair.

Seemingly daydreaming, the child stepped out of line. "Back in line this instant, Laurel!" The matron's sharp voice crackled. She jerked the child by her shoulder back into the line.

Anna was indignant. That was unnecessary, she thought. Then she saw a third girl with braided brown pigtails slip her hand over and pat Laurel's shoulder.

Anna's heart warmed at this small unnoticed act of comfort. As if sensing her sympathy, the child looked at Anna. Anna drew in a breath, almost stunned by the sad but beautiful eyes. At that moment, the sound of the matron's wood clapper sent the line forward.

In that brief moment, something had happened that moved Anna deeply. For the first time in this entire year of talking about them, these orphans who were her husband's cause became real to her. They were individuals, each different, separate, with hearts and minds and souls of their own. Each had a history, a story to tell, a life to live. Maybe now she, Anna Maury Scott, could be a part of it.

"Miss Clinock will see you now. Come in, please," a voice announced.

Gripped by her new insight, Anna took a seat beside her husband in the neat but stark office of Greystone's head matron.

"They must be in good health and old enough to take care of themselves, things like dressing and hygiene."

Matthew presented the requirements for the orphans to travel on the Orphan Train. "They must be reasonably intelligent and capable of understanding this opportunity."

"And how many from Greystone will you be able to handle?" Miss Clinock held her ink pen poised over a paper bearing a long list of names.

"On this trip we're limited to fifteen children from each of the four institutions who are sending children West."

"Only fifteen?" The matron tapped the tip of her pen on her bottom teeth. "But so many need homes—"

"I know." Anna's husband shook his head sadly. "But our resources are limited, and only two railroad cars have been donated to us, one for boys and one for girls. Contributions to our society are our main funding, Miss Clinock, and we have to figure in food and emergency expenses."

He paused. "We expect to be helped out by the adopting families and the churches where we'll be stopping. They're planning to have a kind of Orphan Train Day. They'll be serving meals and giving the families time to meet and get to know the children."

Miss Clinock's eyes peered above the top of the half glasses that pinched her nose. "Then you do expect all of the children to be adopted?"

"At each stop, the children who are selected will go home with their new parents. The rest will get back on the train and go on. And yes, that is our prayer."

Anna watched the head matron sitting in her chair at the desk. Her expression did not betray any emotion.

"As you may know, Reverend Scott, Greystone is largely a shelter for very young abandoned and orphaned children. We do not keep children after they enter their teens.

"At that time boys go to the Poor Boys' Home over in Milltown to work in the cotton mill until they're eighteen and on their own." Miss Clinock's lips pursed together like a straight pin.

"The girls we divide into two classes. We try to find apprenticeships in the trades for the brighter girls, and the rest go into factory work."

Anna's thoughts went back to the three precious little girls in line.

"What I'm saying is, our babies are pretty much in demand and do not stay here long. Neither do those children placed here during a family crisis. They're usually claimed by relatives.

"It's the older children, the ones past the baby stage, who are hard to place. You know, everyone wants a blue-eyed, blond, curly-headed baby girl."

Anna realized from the emotion in the woman's voice that her first impression had been wrong.

The matron forced a smile and rose from her seat. "So, I suggest I pick a few of these children for you to meet. Then we can decide about the best ones for you to take with you on this Orphan Train."

She checked a watch pinned to the lapel of her fitted brown jacket. "They're at recreation now. It's a half hour until their midday meal. This would be a good time for you to see them."

With that, Miss Clinock went to the door, opened it, and motioned them to come with her. As they followed her pencil-slim figure down the corridor, Anna found herself breathing a prayer. She was asking God to let those three little girls be among those chosen for her to shepherd to new homes out West.

5

The Orphan Train

Anna Scott sat reading her Bible by the wavering light of an oil lamp suspended from the rack over her head. She was tired and found it difficult to keep her mind from wandering. They had been traveling for three weeks, and Anna was feeling discouraged.

Keeping the children occupied from early in the morning until late at night was exhausting. At first she had tried to set up some kind of routine for the day. First, they would wash up, have a short devotion and morning prayer. Then she would pass out their breakfast of jam and bread.

Anna had brought along a map of the United States and had pinned it to the train car's wall, showing the children where they were each day and pointing to the next stop. She had taught them a number of games to play in groups, and often she would gather them together to sing hymns as well as lively songs with clapping and some sort of activity. Still, the days were long cooped up in a railroad car, and Anna was weary.

She looked out the window into the blackness. Not even a moon brightened their way tonight. The darkness matched her mood.

She had to admit that the frequent stops to take on food for the dining car and wood and coal helped. She would bundle the children up and march them along the platform for fresh air and exercise. If the stop was long enough and there was a nearby field, she encouraged a game of tag or run-sheep-run. At least this helped them release some of their pent-up energy.

Anna had also brought along some books so she could read aloud to the girls in their railroad car at night before bedtime. And during each evening prayer, she would end with the sincere cry of her heart, that each child would find a loving home.

Of the sixty children who had accompanied them from Boston, thirty had been little girls. Eleven of them still remained. Only two more towns were left as scheduled stops. What if some of these are left and not adopted? What would she and Matthew do? Anna could not think about that now.

She raised her head, feeling the tension in her neck and shoulders. In some of the towns only a few people had come forward to claim their adopted children. And they were farm families needing extra hands and wanting mostly boys. But these little girls needed homes too.

Anna sighed as she looked down at the Bible on her lap. She had been searching through the psalms, seeking verses of encouragement. But now the words on the page had begun to blur.

She blinked her tired eyes and looked down the length of the darkened car.

At night the backs of the seats were turned down and over, made into beds with pillows and blankets spread over them. Most of the children were sound asleep now.

Just then she heard the muffled sound of giggles from the far corner of the car. Anna stifled a smile. Maybe she should get up, go over to them, and reprimand them.

But, on second thought, what harm were they doing? They weren't disturbing anyone.

For a minute, her eyes rested on the three little heads so close together. From the first, she had bonded with the trio she had seen that day in the hall at Greystone. Kit's shiny brown hair adorned the head of a child of such sweetness and generosity. Laurel's tangle of dark hair framed a beautiful little face. And of course, there was Toddy with her golden-red mop of ringlets, who kept everyone guessing what she was going to do next.

Anna frowned. It puzzled her that none of these three had yet been adopted. They were certainly among the most winsome of all the girls. They had everything an adoptive parent would want. Who would not fall in love with one of them? Yet at stop after stop, they reboarded the train with the other unselected ones. Anna simply could not understand why.

Just then the murmur of voices grew louder, followed by a peal of light laughter. She knew she must act quickly before they awakened the other children. She made her way down the aisle between the rows of sleeping bodies.

"You girls must quiet down immediately." She tried to make her whisper sound stern. "You'll wake up the others."

She tucked their blankets around them. "You need a good night's sleep. Tomorrow's a big day."

The train car suddenly jerked, and Mrs. Scott reached for one of the overturned seats to steady herself as she made her way back. She wished she could discuss her feelings with Matthew. But he was in the other car with the boys, and there was no passageway between. He probably had his hands full with problems of his own anyway.

During the entire journey, she and her husband had had little chance to say more than a few words to one another. They each were busy with their charges. And at the train stops, they usually were dealing with questions from adoptive parents.

And some of them asked the most outrageous questions! Anna's cheeks almost burned when she thought about it. They would stand right in front of the children and think nothing of saying something like, "That one's too thin. I want one bigger." Or "How did this child get such ugly brown hair?"

It made Anna so furious she often had to send up a hurried prayer for forgiveness at her thoughts. And these folks were supposed to be Christians!

As she prepared to settle down on her own narrow bed, a preview of tomorrow's scene flashed through her mind. She would make sure they looked their very best—hair neat, faces scrubbed, shoes shined. Then the children would get off the train and line up on the platform where the townspeople usually waited. Even for Anna, this inspection was an ordeal. She could only imagine what it must be like for the children.

Matthew would talk with the person in charge, usually the minister or a member of the city council. Her hands would be full just keeping the children together.

Anna bunched up her pillow, curled herself on the makeshift mattress, and tried to sleep. But sleep did not come easily. For some reason, those three little faces kept her awake tonight.

Tomorrow, she determined, she was going to pay special attention to these "Three Musketeers." She would try to figure out the riddle of why they weren't being selected for adoption.

The following morning the train chugged into Springview puffing steam. Its whistle tooted loudly. A crowd of people clustered on the depot platform craning their necks as the train screeched to a stop.

Anna busily scurried the children into a line. "Remember, be pleasant and polite," she coached them. "And above all, smile!"

Toddy, Laurel, and Kit stood together.

"Now, don't forget, Kit. You be sure to turn your foot sideways and drag it so you'll limp." Toddy kept her voice at a whisper. Turning to Laurel, she instructed, "Remember, hunch up your shoulders, one higher than the other. And twist your mouth. See? Like this." She modeled an awful expression.

Laurel tried to mimic her, but Toddy wrinkled her brow in doubt.

"Try to stay behind me like you can't walk on your own. And I'll—how's this?" When the youngster crossed her eyes, her two friends clapped their hands over their mouths to hide their escaping giggles.

"Careful!" Toddy issued a warning. "This has got to work!"

The wives of the Springview City Council had organized refreshments. Before long, everyone had gathered inside the town hall.

One of the women cornered Anna for a chat. As they were talking, another woman burst in.

"I must say, Mrs. Scott, I understood these orphans were healthy, strong, and ready to work in our homes and fields. I think it is awful to try to palm off such misfits like these crippled children on decent folks!"

"I—I don't know what you mean," stammered Anna. "The children are well. They're perfectly able to do house work and farm work, within reason."

"Then what do you call those three!" The woman stepped aside and pointed across the room.

Anna gasped. Kit was limping toward Toddy with a plate full of food. Just behind her hovered Laurel, her back hunched over and shoulder raised. Toddy sat slumped in a chair along the wall, with her eyes crossed and the most horrible expression on her face.

Her jaw set like cement, Anna started toward the three girls.

"Just what do you think you're doing?"

Before they could answer, Anna heard Matthew's voice. "Anna, this couple is ready to take Stan!"

"We'll see about this later!" she promised the trio.

Once back on the train, she confronted them.

"Why?" she asked. "Why would you do such a naughty thing?"

The girls didn't say a word.

"Isn't anyone going to tell me the truth?" she demanded. "You each know it's sinful to tell lies. Well, you were acting a lie, pretending something that wasn't true. That's just as bad. Why on earth would three perfectly healthy little girls want to look any other way?"

"Because we didn't want to get adopted!" Toddy finally burst out.

"Not want to be adopted?" exclaimed Anna. "But that's the purpose of our whole trip! You were picked out of dozens of other children at Greystone who would've given anything to come. And now you say you don't want to be adopted!"

A long pause followed. Anna waited. It was Kit who broke the silence.

"We don't want to be adopted *separately*, Mrs. Scott."

"We've made a pact to be friends forever," Laurel chimed in. "We want to get adopted in the same town."

"So we've waited until the last town." Toddy tilted her head to one side and turned up the palms of her small hands to explain.

"So that's it," Anna replied, trying to remain stern. "Who's idea was this game?"

Toddy hung her head, but there was a mischievious twinkle in her eyes.

"That was very, very naughty, Toddy," Anna said severely. Then she turned to the other two. "But going along with it was just as naughty," she scolded. "Remember what happened in the Garden of Eden? Adam sinned as much as Eve when he ate the forbidden fruit. He could have refused, but he didn't. So, you see, you are each to blame."

By now, the railroad car was slowly rocking as the engine pulled it away from the Springview station.

Anna ushered the girls to their seats.

"Mrs. Scott, there's just one more town, isn't there?" Toddy raised her little voice against the clanging and creaking. "We won't do it again."

The other two wriggled in their seats, agreeing wholeheartedly.

"You see, we had to be sure. It was the only way we could be sure we'd get to stay together."

Meadowridge

"If I may say so, Mrs. Hale, you may live to regret this."

The longtime housekeeper watched her mistress put on her bonnet.

"You may certainly say so, Clara, but I don't agree." Olivia pushed the long pin through the hat band and into her neatly coiled bun. "I think it's the best thing I can do for Helene. You've heard her yourself, dozens of times. Her dearest wish is for a little sister."

"But ma'am, what kind of child will you get from an Orphan Train?" The expression on Clara's face showed real concern. "I've heard they drag the city streets for these children. And you want to bring one here into this house to live with Miss Helene."

With her hat in place, Mrs. Hale turned away from the front hall mirror. "I've outlined very clearly what kind of child we need, Clara. Mr. and Mrs. Scott understand our situation." She picked up her long kid gloves and started to put them on, carefully smoothing each finger. "Besides, Helene will make the final selection."

Clara folded her arms on the starched bosom of her crisp white apron and sniffed.

"And I might add, Clara, that this child is to be treated like one of the family. Do I make myself clear?"

"Yes, ma'am, very clear."

"Good." Mrs. Hale took one more glance in the mirror. "Now, please go and see if Miss Tuttle has Helene ready for the drive to the train station."

The housekeeper started up the stairs but paused for a final word. "You know I'm not the only one. Miss Tuttle is upset about this too." Clara frowned and headed up the stairs.

Mrs. Hale finished buttoning her gloves thoughtfully. She too had some doubts, but she wasn't going to share them with her housekeeper. Was she doing the right thing, bringing in a stranger to live as a companion to her granddaughter? Helene had been thrilled at the idea, so now there was no turning back. Olivia only hoped to heaven that Clara was wrong.

Muted voices floated down the long curved staircase.

"You mustn't hurry so, Helene." Miss Tuttle's warning carried into the downstairs foyer.

Dressed in a stylish coat and ribboned bonnet, Helene came down the stairs. She looked pale, but her eyes were shining. "Oh, Grandmother, it's really time, isn't it! I can hardly wait to see her. I wish they'd sent a picture. But that's all right. I'll know her right away. I know I will!"

"Now, Helene!" Miss Tuttle shook her head so that the stiff wings of her white nurse's cap fluttered. "All of this excitement isn't good for you."

"Mrs. Hale, do you think she should go down to the train station with all that crowd, all that confusion?" The nurse still held on to Helene's arm. Clara stood to one side.

Olivia looked at her slender, dark-haired granddaughter. Her pallor was worrisome, but she had never seen Helene so happy.

"Oh, Grandmother," Helene protested. "Please, I want to go! I have to go!"

"I think it would be far worse for her to stay at home when she's been looking forward so much to this day." Olivia spoke directly to Miss Tuttle. Ignoring the nurse's sour expression, she said, "Of course you're going, dear."

"Oh, thank you, Grandmother. See, Miss Tuttle, it's all right. I feel perfectly fine. And I want to be there when my little sister gets off the train."

"Well then, Clara, tell Jepson to bring the carriage around. We want to get to the station in plenty of time before the train arrives." Olivia's order was firm.

"I've got her present, Grandmother. I hope she likes it." Helene held up a brightly wrapped package with a big red bow.

"I'm sure she will." Olivia smiled fondly at the child.

Because of her illness, Helene was small for her age. Her eyes seemed too big for her thin face, but her smile was radiant. She was so like her father. Olivia's heart melted each time she saw that smile. If only Helene had inherited her father's strength and stamina. Many times she had listened to the dire warnings of Helene's nurse. But not today. So what if the excitement meant Helene would have to stay in bed for a few days. It would be well worth it to see her so happy.

The ladies of the Meadowridge Community Church had prepared a feast in the church social hall. Some of the recipes had been prize winners at the county fair: platters of fried chicken, sliced ham, steaming meat loaf, bowls of coleslaw, potato salad, homemade bread and rolls still warm from the oven. Cherry, apple, and blueberry pies, a walnut bundt cake, a lemon pound cake, and two chocolate layer cakes covered the crisp blue-checkered tablecloths.

Everything looked delicious. Toddy, Laurel, and Kit found their mouths watering as the wonderful aroma of freshly cooked foods reached them. For days at a time, their daily menu had been crackers, jam, dried apples, and oatmeal cooked on the small potbellied stove at one end of the railroad car. Sometimes Mrs. Scott had handed out a few hard candies as a treat. Only once in a while, during a long stop, was Pastor Scott able to purchase some fresh milk and fruit.

The children stood staring, wide-eyed. Finally, one church lady stepped forward and pushed them gently into line along with the other orphans. While the children treated themselves in the center of the room, church families watched and murmured to one another along the side walls of the social hall.

The girls sat beside each other on three straight-backed chairs placed around the walls, eating their meal. Because Toddy's feet did not quite reach the floor, she hung her heels over the rung to steady herself as she ate. Balancing her plate on her knees was not an easy task, especially when she could feel the eyes of other people looking at her.

From the time Miss Clinock had assembled them in her office to tell them what was going to happen, Toddy had been very excited. She could talk of little else. She had long ago given up hope that her mother would ever show up, but her vivid imagination never allowed her to give up hope for a magical happy ending. She had packed and repacked the small cardboard suitcase issued for the trip. The idea of traveling hundreds of miles by train to a new town out West and being adopted by a real family sounded like the greatest of adventures to her.

Glancing up from her plate, Toddy spotted a girl in a pretty blue dress on the other side of the room. Her dark hair was drawn back from her pale face with a large bow.

Her eyes seemed very big, and she was smiling—right at Toddy!

Anna Scott stood at the doorway surveying the scene. Matthew and Reverend Brewster, the minister of the Meadowridge Community Church, were talking at a table at one end of the hall. In front of them were all the children's papers containing their vital statistics—birth dates; natural parents' names, if known; place of birth; release forms for adoption. After making their choices, the adoptive parents would go there to sign the papers.

Mrs. Scott was concerned. She had not been able to tell her husband about the three little girls. She wanted to help them fulfill their hearts' desire. She started to make her way toward him before any of the papers were signed.

However, a woman introducing herself as the chairman of the ladies guild stopped her.

"I wasn't sure whether you knew that we have many families from outside Meadowridge that come here to church," she said gaily. "We sent out announcements about your Orphan Train, Mrs. Scott, so I feel sure people will be arriving all day with plans to take one of these poor little ones."

Anna felt a stab of alarm. What if these families took one of the little girls? They would hardly ever see each other, much less attend school together. She must make sure that didn't happen. She had to speak to Matthew. Hurriedly excusing herself, Anna scurried on.

She had taken only a few steps when a voice halted her. "One minute, if you please, Mrs. Scott."

Anna turned as the handsome woman, elegantly dressed in fashionable black, placed a gloved hand on her arm.

"I'm Olivia Hale," she said. "You may remember that you and your husband came to tea at my home on your last visit to Meadowridge."

At her words Anna recalled the day vividly. The enormous hilltop house. The magnificent parlor. The silver pot and delicate china cups.

"I invited you to discuss my adopting a child, a girl, to be a companion to my granddaughter, Helene."

Anna felt flush, recalling her less than charitable attitude toward the woman.

"She doesn't want a child," Anna had told her husband. "She wants a doll that talks and breathes and can play!"

Anna smiled at the lady as the memory instantly flooded back into her mind. Immediately she thought of one of her special three, Kit Ternan. Kit, with her sweet quiet ways and gentle warmth, would make an ideal companion for the invalid girl. But before she could voice her suggestion, a dark-haired girl in blue was tugging at Mrs. Hale's arm.

"Oh, Grandmother, I've found her!" she exclaimed. "My little sister. Look, Grandmother, over there! See?"

Anna turned to follow the direction of the granddaughter's pointed finger. To her amazement, it was Toddy.

Within moments, Helene had happily taken Toddy's little hand and drawn her to one side. Excitedly, she began telling her about all the wonderful things she had planned for the two of them to do. Mrs. Hale and Mrs. Scott walked toward the adoption table.

"Toddy is a delightful child, Mrs. Hale, cheerful and bright. I think she will be a wonderful companion for your granddaughter."

"Not too lively?"

Anna Scott laughed. "Well, she's certainly not dull."

The more she thought about it, the more she realized that Toddy was the right one. For a lonely child such as Helene, sentenced to a life of limited activity, Toddy would breathe a breath of fresh air into the days.

Mrs. Hale shook her head as she looked over the background information on the child Helene had chosen. She read:

Name of child: Zephronia Victorine Todd
Birth date: June 1882
Female, White; Hair, Red-gold; Eyes, Blue; Health, Excellent
Mother: Mazel Cooper   Occupation: Dancer
Last known address: Rialto Theater, Boston, Massachusetts. No communication since 1888. Child transferred from "temporary" status to "available for placement" January 1890.
Father: John Todd
Occupation: Comedic actor, song and dance, Haynes Vaudeville Troupe
Present whereabouts: unknown

Mrs. Hale picked up the pen on the table near Matthew Scott and signed the form. Whatever she had gotten herself into, she was determined to see it through. As the Good Book said, having set her hand to the plow, she would not look back. One glance at her granddaughter's smiling face was enough to convince her that this was the only decision she could have made.

A short while later, the twosome was settled in the carriage opposite Mrs. Hale.

"Oh, Grandmother, isn't Toddy cunning?

Turning to Toddy, she said, "Oh, Toddy, I'm so glad you've come. I've wanted a little sister for so long. We're going to have the most wonderful times together."

Reacting at once to Helene's excitement, Toddy gave a little bounce. Soon they were both laughing merrily.

Mrs. Hale could not keep her own mouth from lifting in amusement at the two children's delight with each other. Maybe it was going to be fine after all, in spite of Clara's feelings about bringing a strange child into their lives and Miss Tuttle's endless displeasure about Helene's activities. As she watched the two girls, however, she had the strong feeling that the Hale household was in for a big change.

7

The first thing Toddy saw when she entered the Hale house was a tall woman dressed in white standing by the staircase in the front hall, her arms folded and her foot tapping impatiently.

"Helene looks very flushed, Mrs. Hale. It's my opinion she should go straight to bed and have supper on a tray. I refuse to take responsibility if she has any more excitement this evening."

The stiff peaked cap moved as she shook her head back and forth. The stranger hurried to Helene's side to help her off with her coat.

"But I'm not tired, Miss Tuttle," Helene protested. "And I don't want to leave Toddy on her first night here. Look, isn't she a darling?"

Toddy smiled at the white lady, but a cold hard stare met her. In one chilling moment, Toddy recognized an enemy. This woman did not like her.

Pulling off her gloves, Mrs. Hale looked at her granddaughter anxiously. Helene did have unusually high color in her cheeks. There was no use taking any chances. After all, she did pay Miss Tuttle a handsome salary to take care of her. She would have to rely on her judgment.

"Oh, Grandmother!" wailed Helene. "I feel fine, really I do. Let me stay up for dinner at least! Then I'll go straight to bed. I promise."

The young girl's pleading eyes echoed the cry. Mrs. Hale hesitated.

"Well, just until dinner. But then you must go to bed. There'll be plenty of time for the two of you to be together. Toddy is going to be living here from now on. You don't want to be ill tomorrow and not be able to enjoy her company, do you?"

Helene's eyes sparkled. "Oh, thank you, Grandmother. Come along, Toddy. I want to show you the playroom. We got you some toys and games." Helene took Toddy's hand and started upstairs.

"Slowly, Helene," Miss Tuttle cautioned, hurrying after them. "Don't rush!"

Ignoring the nurse's frown, Olivia turned away. Only time would tell if she had made a terrible mistake. Right now all she could see was the happiness in Helene's eyes. She was not going to borrow trouble.

An hour later the three of them sat in the candlelit dining room at a long table with a creamy linen tablecloth. Gleaming silverware and crystal glasses had been set at each place. Toddy's eyes grew large with the newness of what was happening.

At Greystone, she had lined up with the others and passed along the serving counter with her plate while her food was dished out to her. There were no choices and no seconds.

Here, a man in a dark jacket moved silently back and forth between a huge table nearby and the dining room table. Mrs. Hale called the man Thomas and the table a buffet. He carried different covered silver serving dishes to them. First he would take one to Mrs. Hale and then the same one to Helene. Each of them helped themselves. When he approached Toddy with a platter of pork chops, she hesitated.

"Would you like me to serve you, miss?" he asked quietly.

She nodded shyly. "Yes, please."

The gentleman used a silver utensil. It was a fork and spoon connected in the middle. He picked up a chop and placed it on her plate.

After that came a silver bowl with a mountain of snowy potatoes and valley of melted butter. Each time, Thomas would offer her the serving dish for a few seconds. Toddy knew he was allowing her time to decide if she could serve herself. She felt relieved to be getting the help.

When Thomas arrived with a covered dish of piping hot rolls, Toddy gave him one of her best smiles. His expression remained the same, although Toddy thought she saw one of the kind man's eyelids drop briefly in a wink.

At last, he brought them dessert. To Toddy's delight, it was creamy caramel custard in a pretty crystal dish.

"Thomas, I'll take my coffee in the parlor this evening," Mrs. Hale said as she placed her napkin beside her empty dessert plate. "Time for you to go up now, Helene."

Toddy could almost feel Miss Tuttle's presence before she appeared in the dining room doorway to get Helene.

Helene slowly slipped from her chair, went over to Toddy, and hugged her.

"Good night, Toddy. I'll see you in the morning." At the door, she paused and looked back longingly. "I'm so glad you're here!"

After Helene had left, Mrs. Hale rose and pushed back her chair, its legs scraping across the wooden floor. "Come along, Toddy, we need to get acquainted."

A cheerful fire was burning in the fireplace, the curtains had been drawn, and the lamps on the marble-topped tables had been lighted. Mrs. Hale took a seat in one of the chairs by the fireplace and motioned for Toddy to take the matching one on the other side. Toddy silently crawled into the big chair.

"Toddy, there are a few things you must remember now that you'll be living here. The first is Helene. Although she may look fine to you, she has a very weak heart and must not get overexcited. So you'll have to be careful what games you play with her. Sometimes she extends herself too far, and we have to summon the doctor."

Toddy had folded her hands in her lap while she listened. She nodded her little head.

"Mrs. Scott told me you are a very smart little girl. So I'm relying on you to follow my orders. Miss Tuttle is Helene's nurse, so you'll have to obey her orders too. Remember, it's for Helene's good."

"Yes, ma'am, I'll remember." Toddy scrunched up her face very seriously.

"Good."

The parlor door opened, and Thomas brought in a tray with a silver coffee pot and china cup and saucer. He set it down on the table in front of Mrs. Hale.

"Will there be anything else, ma'am?"

"Not for me, Thomas. But ask Mrs. Hubbard to come in, please."

After Thomas had left, she said to Toddy, "It's been a long day for all of us and especially for you, Toddy. So I think it's time for bed. Our housekeeper will show you to your room. It's right next to Helene's. She's probably asleep by now, so you won't disturb her, will you?"

Toddy shook her red head just as a knock sounded at the door.

"Come in, Clara," Mrs. Hale called. A stout, gray-haired woman bustled in. Toddy had not seen her before. She cast an unsmiling face in Toddy's direction.

"Mrs. Hubbard, this is Toddy, who will be staying with us, as you know. Would you kindly take her upstairs and help her get settled?"

"Yes, ma'am." The woman turned and walked briskly to the door. "Come along," she told Toddy.

"Good night, Toddy. Sleep well," Mrs. Hale called out as the child followed the housekeeper out of the room.

Mrs. Hubbard never looked back to see if anyone was behind her. She just marched up the wide staircase. Toddy had to hurry to keep up. At the landing she made a turn and went down a long corridor. At the end, she paused at a door and held it open.

The bedroom was huge, the biggest one Toddy had ever seen. And it was beautiful. A high bed with ruffled pillows caught her eye. Long curtains, made out of the same material as the flowered cushions on the two chairs, had been pulled over a curved bank of windows. A dresser with a tall mirror completed the furnishings.

"Well, I suppose you have something to sleep in, don't you?" Mrs. Hubbard had already turned down the crocheted coverlet on the high bed and was fluffing up the pillows.

Toddy started toward her battered suitcase.

"What kind of name is Toddy anyway?" Mrs. Hubbard snapped.

"My mother called me Toddy," the little girl explained. "But my real name is Zephronia Victorine."

At this the housekeeper threw up her hands. "For mercy sakes! What can people be thinkin' of to dream up a name like that!"

Toddy lifted her wrinkled flannel nightie out of the suitcase.

"No, that will never do! You can't wear that rag into a bed that's just been made up fresh. You'll have to wear one of Helene's, even if it does swallow you up." The housekeeper put her hands on her hips. "I think you'll be needing a bath too."

The woman saw the child's face redden. Clara Hubbard had disapproved of the plan to take in an orphan. But the little one was here now, and Clara would just have to make the best of it. After all, it wasn't the child's fault she was an orphan, and it also wasn't her fault that her clothes were wrinkled.

"Wait till you see the bathroom!" This time her words had a lilt to them.

Five minutes later, the little girl was floating in the biggest tub she had ever seen, amid warm white soapy bubbles. The tub had lion's claw legs and sat on a platform. Beside it stood a porcelain washbowl on a pedestal and a rack with thick towels embroidered with the initials *OH*.

Using a soft sponge, Mrs. Hubbard scrubbed Toddy until she was pink and tingling all over. After a shampoo and dry, the housekeeper dropped a sweet-smelling, lace-trimmed nightgown over Toddy's head.

Toddy climbed up into the bed and sank into the feathery mattress.

"Well, then, you're all settled." The housekeeper was smiling as she surveyed Toddy's situation. "Next time, you can do for yourself." She spread a colored quilt over the girl, then picked up the lamp and went to the door. "So, good night to you."

The housekeeper's firm footsteps faded away, and then everything was quiet. Too quiet. In fact, the deep silence seemed eerie. For the first time in her life, Toddy was alone.

Used to the sound of others breathing or coughing or turning in their squeaky bedsprings, the little girl had never slept by herself. And she didn't like it now. She missed Laurel and Kit. She wondered where each of them was tonight. Were they lonely? Did they miss her as much as she missed them?

A stinging rush of tears filled her eyes and rolled down her cheeks. Quickly, she turned over to bury her head in the soft, lavender-scented pillow and cry.

It'll be all right, she told herself. She was Helene's little sister now, and tomorrow she would see Helene again. Tomorrow would be the beginning of the "happily ever after" that Toddy had always longed for.

8

Whatever Toddy had expected her life to be, she soon discovered it was not going to be a fairy tale. The day after Toddy arrived, Helene awakened with a fever, and Mrs. Hale had to send for Dr. Woodward. There was a great deal of rushing up and down the halls as Miss Tuttle issued orders.

Miss Tuttle made it known to Toddy and everyone else what she felt about Helene's fever. The trip to the train station to pick up Toddy had been too much. Bringing home this orphan was the problem.

For the next few days everything in the Hale residence centered on Helene. Meals were served in the small morning room beside the big dining room where Toddy had eaten the first night. Nobody paid particular attention to the little girl. Mrs. Hale remained distant, and Toddy only caught glimpses of her, mostly as she paced the upstairs hall outside Helene's room..

But Toddy knew how to take care of herself, so she found things to do. This wasn't very hard since Helene had already made sure there were many new books and games. The trouble was that most of the games required a partner.

Toddy wandered about, wishing more than ever that she knew exactly where Kit and Laurel had been "placed out."

The afternoon of the second day, the youngster became restless. It was a beautiful sunny day and much too nice to stay inside. Toddy decided to go exploring, so she slipped down the stairs and out the side door into the garden.

To her amazement, the garden was as big as the playground at Greystone. Gravel paths wound their way through colorful blooming flower beds. Toddy had never seen so many different kinds of flowers. She recognized some from the arrangement in the bowl in the center of the dining room table. Others she had seen in vases throughout the house. She walked around, stopping to touch them gently, bending down here and there to smell their sweet scent.

All of a sudden, she spotted a man in overalls. He was busily trimming the hedges against the spiked iron fence at the garden's outside edge. Eager to talk to someone, Toddy skipped over to him.

"Hello!" she greeted cheerfully.

The man scowled at her and went on snipping with his wide, pointed shears.

"I've come to live here."

Still no answer.

"I came all the way 'cross country in a train."

Another grunt. The snippers moved without stopping.

"My name's Toddy. What's yours?"

"Ferrin," the gardener growled.

"I'm going to be Helene's little sister." Toddy moved along with him as he went to the next hedge.

"You're one of them orphans, ain't you?" he turned and gave her a hard look.

"Yes!" she smiled.

"Well, I wouldn't be gettin' no fancy ideas if I wuz you," he said. "Blood's thicker 'n water. Make no mistake 'bout that."

Toddy was puzzled. What did he mean? she wondered. As Ferrin moved forward, she fell into step beside him.

"Now, you go along with you! I'm busy!" The sound of the snippers stopped for a moment. "Don't have time for gabbin'. Got my work to do."

Toddy shrugged and whirled around to start down a path in the opposite direction. She'd just have to find something else to do.

There, at the far end of the garden was an elaborate gazebo with white lattice and a pointed roof. Curious, Toddy headed for it. What a wonderful place to play in, she thought when she walked inside. She could do little skits and pantomimes, just like a real theater. If only she had someone to do it with.

Just then a head of tawny hair peered over the fence.

"Who are you?" Toddy gasped, startled by the boy's sudden appearance.

"I'm Chris Blanchard. Who are you?"

"I'm Toddy. What are you doing there?"

"Oh, I'm climbing trees in ole Mr. Traherne's orchard. What are you doing there?"

"I live here."

"Since when? Nobody but rich ole Mrs. Hale lives in *that* house."

"Not anymore. I live here, and so does Helene."

"Who's Helene?"

"My sister. We're sisters, and I do so live here!"

The boy scrunched up his face as if he were considering that fact. Then he asked. "Wanna play?"

This was exactly what Toddy wanted to do. "Sure!"

"Can you climb trees?"

"Of course."

"Well, come on then."

The gnarled, twisted trees in Traherne's apple orchard proved great fun. Toddy and her new friend climbed one low branch after the other. They ran around the trunks, playing tag and laughing. Chris even shared some crumbled gingerbread he had stashed in his pocket. They soon found out they were the same age and in September would both be in Miss Cady's third grade class at Meadowridge Grammar School.

Toddy didn't know how much time had passed when she heard the sound of a voice calling her name. "Toddy! Toddy!"

"Good-bye, Chris!"

The girl hurriedly scrambled down from a tree, back over the fence, and into the garden. There she found Mrs. Hubbard with her arms folded in front, glaring at her.

"Well, if you aren't a sight!" the housekeeper declared. "We've been looking all over for you. Mrs. Hale's been worried."

Toddy felt bad. She had never thought to ask permission. Even if she was in trouble, the afternoon had been worth it. Chris was fun, for a boy.

"She thought you'd run away or something. Well, come along." Mrs. Hubbard opened up the back door. "Let's get you cleaned up. Helene's feeling better and has been asking for you."

The woman took Toddy by the arm and pulled her along to the house.

"More trouble than it's worth!" Mrs. Hubbard mumbled as she swiped the dirt off Toddy's face with a damp washcloth. "And what in the world will we put on you?"

Toddy wanted Mrs. Hubbard to like her, to be her friend, so she looked into her frowning face, smiled sweetly, and said, "I'm sorry."

Slowly the icy look in the housekeeper's face thawed.

"Oh well, children will be children, I suppose," Clara sighed. There *was* something angelic about that little face, she had to admit. "Now, you're presentable, so go along with you. Helene's been frettin' to see you."

Miss Tuttle stood like an iron guard in front of Helene's door. She shook her finger sternly. "Now, young lady, you are not to tire Helene out. Understand?"

"Yes, ma'am."

The nurse opened the bedroom door. Miss Tuttle was mean, and Toddy knew the nurse would probably never like her. But when Toddy saw Helene's welcoming smile, she forgot everything else.

Dr. Woodward had ordered Helene to stay in bed for the rest of the week. In spite of Miss Tuttle's advice against it, Toddy was allowed to spend a good deal of time with her. This was mostly because Helene had insisted on it and Mrs. Hale had consented.

Helene's room was the grandest bedroom the little girl had ever seen, decorated all in pink roses. Toddy loved to sink her stocking feet into its thick, soft, green carpet. Sometimes she'd even play hopscotch on the rug's pattern of roses and try to skip across the room to the tall curtained windows with their tied-back pink bows. The room blossomed like Mr. Ferrin's flower garden with roses in the wallpaper and on the glass shade covering the tall lamp on Helene's pink marble-topped bedside table.

And then there were the books. Toddy had never seen so many books at one time. Helene's room was like the library at the orphanage but much nicer. When the two girls were alone, Helene would read to Toddy, and the little girl loved it. Helene's voice was kind and gentle, but she could roar like a lion or squeal like a mouse when she read from a book. Toddy would giggle, and Helene would animate the story all the more.

Helene also loved Bible stories. Each one came alive to Toddy through Helene's reading. The story of David and Goliath or Moses and the Ten Commandments were two of Toddy's favorites. Helene knew exactly how to bring them to life. Sometimes Mrs. Hale would even let the two girls stay up for a while after bedtime to finish one.

Since Helene wasn't strong enough to attend regular school, a lady called a tutor came to teach her at home. Toddy loved to spin the large globe on top of the long table in front of the bookcases while Helene told her about such faraway places as China and Japan. Helene seemed to know something about everything because she had read so much.

"You know, Toddy, I'm an orphan too," Helene confided one day as they played Parcheesi propped against the mounds of ruffled pillows on the high, shiny brass bed. "If it weren't for Grandmother, I would probably have been put in an orphanage just like you."

Sitting cross-legged, Toddy rolled her dice and then looked at Helene. She wanted to tell Helene that her parents weren't really dead, but she bit her tongue. The little girl had long ago given up hope that her mother would return to get her. And two years at Greystone had erased many of her memories anyway. Every once in a while, mostly when she was drifting off to sleep at night, Toddy would remember something about her former life—a snatch of a song she had learned listening from the wings of the theater stage or a flash of a dance she had seen over and over. But for the most part these memories had faded then almost vanished completely.

"So did you have many friends there?" Helene seemed genuinely interested in Toddy's life at the orphanage.

"I had two special ones," Toddy replied as she carefully chose which yellow game pieces to move the six spaces. "Kit and Laurel. They got placed out here too."

The look on Toddy's face must have given away her feelings because Helene quickly added, "Do you know where they are, Toddy? I'm sure Grandmother could find out."

Toddy's big blue eyes widened. Her heart actually skipped a beat. "Oh, Helene, could she really?"

"Of course!" Helene quickly shook the dice holder and tossed the dice. "Maybe we could even have them over to play!"

At that, Toddy got so excited she started bouncing, nearly upsetting the Parcheesi board. They both laughed.

"You'll like them, Helene! They're a lot of fun."

As the two girls picked up the markers, Toddy added, "At Greystone we—" She leaned forward on the bed and lowered her voice. "Want me to tell you a secret?"

Helene bobbed her head up and down. "Yes! I love secrets."

"Promise you won't tell anyone—" Toddy thought a moment—"well, it might not matter. Mrs. Scott found out on the train anyway."

Toddy described the girls' plan for staying together. "It was so funny watching that lady in Springview," she giggled.

"I'll bet it was all your idea too, wasn't it?" Helene laughed.

Toddy's dimples showed. "But we had to do it, Helene. At Greystone we promised each other we'd be friends forever. There wasn't any other way."

The next Sunday, Helene was still running a low-grade fever, so she could not attend church.

"I have a surprise for you," she told Toddy as she retrieved two boxes hidden under her mountains of pillows.

Eagerly, Toddy tore into the white tissue paper. In the first was a white straw hat with long blue streamers. In the second box was a matching sailor dress trimmed in dark blue braid with a pleated skirt, a red scarf for the collar, white stockings, and white buttoned shoes.

"Oh, Helene!" Even the thought of Miss Tuttle's scowling face couldn't dampen Toddy's excitement.

"Well, go ahead, try it on!"

Toddy took this as her cue. Without missing a beat, she jammed the straw hat onto her head and began dancing a sailor's jig across the carpet.

> When I was a lad, I served a term,
> As office boy to an Attorney's firm,
> I cleaned the windows and I swept the floor,
> And I polished up the handle of the big front door.
> I polished up the handle so carefulee,
> That now I am the Ruler of the Queen's Navee!

Helene was laughing and clapping her hands to mark the beat.

"I recognize that one, Toddy. It's from *Pinafore*. Grandmother took me to see it when we went to San Francisco last year!"

Encouraged, Toddy was singing and dancing to another verse when all of a sudden a razor-sharp voice sliced through the song. "Stop! Stop that at once!"

Miss Tuttle stood in the doorway, red-faced, bristling. "Need I remind you that this is the Sabbath?"

Toddy stopped dancing.

"And you, Helene. I'm appalled at you for going along with such a vulgar performance. And on Sunday too!"

Miss Tuttle carried a tray of medicine to the bedside.

"But, Miss Tuttle, it was the admiral's song from a Gilbert and Sullivan operetta." Helene came to Toddy's rescue. "Toddy even knew all the words."

Miss Tuttle straightened the wings of her nurse's cap and glared at Toddy. She might have known this little street urchin would pull a stunt like this. Why, the child probably sang for pennies on the streets before she was taken into the orphanage, where she should have remained.

From the first, the nurse had been against taking in one of these waifs. She thought it a foolish risk. An Orphan Train bringing countless children from who knows where, palming them off on gullible people like Mrs. Hale, placing them in decent homes with no thought of the effect. Everything at the Hale house was run according to rules. This child didn't know any rules.

No, this was a big, BIG mistake. And what could you expect from a child whose parents had been, of all things, vaudeville performers! Oh, the shame of it. Such vulgar goings on. Miss Tuttle knew this child would bring disgrace on them all.

Yes, she assured herself as she poured the thick medication into a spoon, Mrs. Hale will certainly see her mistake when she hears about this.

"Take your things to your own room, young lady," Miss Tuttle ordered Toddy. "Finish getting dressed in there."

Toddy quietly gathered the clothes and left.

Within a short time, the nurse saw to it that Mrs. Hale received the report.

"But aren't you even going to reprimand the girl?" Miss Tuttle gasped.

"*Reprimand?*"

"Punish her for breaking the Sabbath! Singing music hall songs and dancing!"

Mrs. Hale took a last sip of morning coffee and replaced her cup in its saucer. "I don't think the incident calls for punishment, Miss Tuttle. Toddy was simply entertaining Helene, and Helene was enjoying it. If I punish one, I must punish the other, and I have no intention of doing either."

"But, madam, aren't you concerned about the bad influence this child is having on Helene?" Miss Tuttle squared her broad shoulders when she talked.

The grandmother stood up. "On the contrary, Miss Tuttle, I think Toddy has been a very good influence on Helene." Her tone was cool. "I've never seen my granddaughter so happy or heard her laugh so much."

A smile softened her mouth as she walked toward the parlor doorway. "I even think the Lord himself might approve. Making a sick child happy is all I see Toddy doing. She's helping Helene in ways all the doctors and medicines and attention can't. Like the Good Book says, Toddy is 'good medicine' for Helene's soul."

After Mrs. Hale had left, Miss Tuttle had to stop herself from storming out behind her. She had never been so humiliated. In other homes where she had done private nursing, her word was law. But Mrs. Hale had dismissed her as if she were nothing more than an ordinary servant. If the position did not pay so well, she would give notice. But, of course, she was totally devoted to Helene. Absolutely devoted to the sick child. No, it was her duty to stay here and try, somehow, to combat the bad influence of this orphan child.

As it turned out, Toddy saw Laurel and Kit sooner than she had expected. When she entered her Sunday school classroom later that same morning, there they both sat!

During snack time, the three girls shared information about their new homes.

"I'm living with the Hansens," Kit told them in her quiet manner. "Their two boys are Caspar and Lonny. They don't like me very much, and there's lots of work to do on their farm. But there's plenty of food, and I have my very own room in the attic. It's got a pretty view too."

Laurel took a swallow of milk to wash down her graham cracker. "I've made a new friend. Her name is Jenny.

She comes three times a week to clean the Woodward's house." Laurel wiped off her milky upper lip with a finger. "The doctor's wife is sad mostly. Jenny says it's because she lost a little girl like me."

Toddy gave her friends all the details about the Hales before they had to line up to go into church for the final hymn and benediction. Then she noticed a young boy with slicked down hair and a stiff white shirt in the boy's line. It was Chris! When she smiled at him, he stuck out his tongue at her. Boys! Toddy shrugged.

After this reunion with her good friends, Toddy looked forward to Sunday school. Sometimes Helene felt well enough to go to church, but she sat with her grandmother for the service because there was no class for her age group. Most of the time, however, Jepson drove only Mrs. Hale and the young Toddy in the grand carriage on Sundays.

By the Fourth of July, Toddy had been at the Hale home nearly six weeks. That morning, the family was eating in the small, sunny breakfast room. A warm breeze flowed through the open windows.

"But Toddy shouldn't miss all the fun just because I can't go, Grandmother. Couldn't Miss Tuttle take her? She could stay with the Woodwards. You know they won't mind. And the parade and games would be so much fun."

"Well, Miss Tuttle does have the day off." The grandmother finished buttering her warm toast. "I could ask her." She lifted the small silver bell by her plate and tinkled it gently. Thomas appeared as if by magic.

"Yes, ma'am?"

"Thomas, would you ask Miss Tuttle to join us for a moment?"

"Yes, ma'am," the butler replied with a slight bow.

A few minutes later, the nurse arrived. Toddy had never seen her in anything but her nurse's uniform. Today, she was dressed in an outfit with a ruffled red and white polka-dot blouse and blue skirt. She looked very different.

"Miss Tuttle, I'd like you to take Toddy along with you over to the park today. After the parade, you can drop her at the Woodwards. She can spend the rest of the day with them."

The strawberry seemed to lodge itself in Toddy's throat as she watched the nurse's expression. Surely Mrs. Hale could see Miss Tuttle didn't want to. Toddy shrank back in her seat. She almost wished she didn't have to go.

Helene's nurse cleared her throat. "Certainly, madam," she replied.

"Thank you. It's settled then. I'll send a note to Mrs. Woodward with you," Mrs. Hale said, picking up her spoon and returning to her dish of strawberries.

Miss Tuttle turned and walked out of the room.

"Are you sure? I mean, I could stay here with you, Helene."

"No, of course not, Toddy. I want you to go. I've been a few times, and it's lots of fun.

"Besides, I have a surprise for you. Grandmother has already worked it out for Laurel and Kit to come over and watch the fireworks with us from the balcony tonight. Won't that be fun?"

The concern in Toddy's face vanished like a thin morning dew on the summer lawn.

Helene laughed. "Go on now. You'd better get ready. Miss Tuttle will want to leave early since it's her day off."

Toddy quickly dashed upstairs to get ready. As she walked out of her room, she nearly ran into Miss Tuttle standing like a statue right in front of her door. Without warning, the tall woman grabbed the little girl's left arm and gave her a good shake.

"Now listen, you little pest!" she hissed as her eyes darted back and forth to see if anyone was coming. "I'm only takin' you as far as the park. I'm meeting a friend and I'm not spoiling my day havin' you tag along. You're plenty big enough to take care of yourself."

Toddy held her breath as long as she could. Her heart was beating so hard it felt like it was going to jump out of her chest.

"And you're not to say a word about this to Mrs. Hale or Helene, you understand?" She squeezed Toddy's arm tighter. "You think you're somethin', comin' in this house and taking over. Well, you're nuthin' but a scrawny theater brat. And I won't have you pulling us all down to your level."

Toddy tried to pull away, but the strong woman only tightened her grip, her nails digging into the child's arm. "Just because Helene has taken a fancy to you doesn't mean you're special. If anything happens to her because of you, I'll see to it that you're out on your ear. You'll end up a beggar. Or maybe you'll wind up singin' for your supper in a backstreet alley or sleeping in a cellar with the rats!"

The nurse's face was as red as the strawberries. "So you'd better listen good or you'll be sorry, do you hear?"

Toddy nodded, feeling the cruel pinch of the woman's spiny fingers bite into her flesh.

"So come on." The nurse had jerked the youngster forward again and started toward the stairs.

As Toddy hurried to follow the nurse down the front staircase, she could still feel the woman's nails in her skin. The places hurt. But they didn't hurt as much as the words. Somehow, the day did not seem as sunny or exciting anymore. She knew Miss Tuttle had meant what she said. Toddy's future at the Hale house was as uncertain as Helene's health.

After breakfast, Helene usually sat on the sun porch and read, but today her grandmother urged her to rest so she could enjoy the night's festivities with the other children. She was in her bedroom when loud whispering in the hallway outside filtered through her half-open door. Much to her horror, she heard every word the nurse said to her beloved Toddy.

"Grandmother. We must do something!"

Olivia stopped arranging the flowers in a vase and looked at her granddaughter.

Helene's face was chalky pale.

"Miss Tuttle was awful, Grandmother. And Toddy's so little!"

Instantly concerned about her granddaughter's health, Olivia put down her clipping shears. "Helene, dear, sit down. What happened?"

Helene told her grandmother everything she had heard.

The next morning when Toddy came downstairs, Miss Tuttle's carrying case and two suitcases were in the front hall. By the time she had finished breakfast, Miss Tuttle was gone.

10

Summer sped into fall and the opening day of school. Helene's delicate health kept her at home, but Mrs. Hale took Toddy for her first day of school. Dressed in a brand new yellow dress, matching hair ribbon, and white shoes, the eight-year-old entered her class at Meadowridge Grammar School.

Immediately, she looked for Laurel and Kit. Laurel was already there, putting her lunch bag inside a wooden desk near a large bank of windows. Kit arrived soon after. Before the teacher rang the small bell on her desk, the three friends had settled close together, each silently hoping Miss Cady would not move them.

At recess that day, the girls went together to eat their lunch under a big oak tree and to watch some of the girls jump rope. Nearby, boys were rolling marbles on the front porch of the school house.

"Where's your mama, little girl?"

Toddy had just bitten into her ham sandwich when she heard the taunting words. She stopped chewing for a moment. Laurel and Kit stopped eating too.

"What's an Orphan Train like anyway?"

A second voice echoed the first. Two boys from Miss Cady's class peeked around the oak tree.

"Bet you can't even read or write!" one of them mocked with his nose in the air.

"Yeh, my ma says you'll probably slow everyone down," the other one jeered.

With that, Toddy's temper flared. She jumped up, her lunch bag dropping to the ground. "You take that back!" she yelled at them, heading toward the tree. "Take it back!" Kit and Laurel watched, stunned.

The boys huddled close and did not budge. "Who's gonna make us?" one of them hooted.

The other one joined in. "Who's gonna make us? Who's gonna make us?"

"I am, that's who!" Toddy was really mad now. She had handled bullies before, and she wasn't afraid. She lunged at the blond-haired one. The boy hollered and leaped to one side. Toddy then aimed at the other one, who shoved her. She landed on the ground.

By now, Toddy's yellow dress and white shoes were covered with dirt. She wiped her mouth with a dirty hand, determined to get these two tormentors if it was the last thing she did.

Just then another voice shouted, "Bill Shepherd! You'd better stop that!" It was Chris Blanchard, the boy who had climbed Mr. Traherne's apple trees with her. In an instant, Chris's fists were punching Bill Shepherd in the chest. Bill jabbed and kicked back as hard as he could.

"Stop this at once!" Miss Cady ordered as Chris took another swipe.

Then the recess bell rang. "You two go to the principal's office. The rest of you get in line. Recess is over."

Late that afternoon, Olivia Hale sat at her desk writing a letter to Anna Scott. She had already sent Anna one progress report on Toddy this past summer. This was the second.

She looked up as Clara came to the parlor door.

"Mrs. Hale, Mrs. Blanchard is here to see you. She doesn't seem too happy."

Olivia put down her pen. "Very well, Clara, please bring her in."

"Now, Olivia—" The words rounded the parlor door before their speaker, "this sort of thing cannot be permitted."

The plump, fashionably dressed woman entered the room.

"Good afternoon, Bernice. So nice to see you. Hasn't it been a beautiful fall day?"

"Olivia, I didn't come to discuss the weather." Mrs. Blanchard plopped down in a nearby armchair. "Now, I realize you've taken in this poor unfortunate orphan. But I won't have her getting my boy into trouble. And that's that!"

"I quite agree, Bernice. I don't want Chris in trouble either. But you must admit, it was an honorable thing for Chris to do. Helping someone in distress, I mean." Olivia's tone was soothing, like ointment on a wound.

Bernice knew that Olivia was trying to mollify her. Perhaps she *had* overreacted. Still, she wanted to make her point in coming.

"Yes, it was. My boy comes from a decent home, and we have tried to set certain standards of behavior . . . It's just that we don't know what kind of influence these *foundlings* could have on our own children. I'm sure you agree we must protect—"

Olivia seemed to be listening, but Bernice wasn't sure she understood how important her son's future was to her. After all, Chris was going places in his life. He'd be attending the university one day, maybe on an athletic scholarship. And of course, he would marry only the most suitable of girls from a socially acceptable family.

"You know I haven't been in favor of this orphan idea from the start, Olivia," Bernice admitted after a pause.

"But I'm willing to set this one incident aside if we can be assured it won't happen again."

Mrs. Blanchard finally left, and Olivia picked up the pen lying on top of her fine stationery. Yes, indeed, with Toddy in the Hale household things were certainly beginning to change.

Fall turned into winter, and before long signs of Christmas were everywhere. Main Street was decorated with red and green garlands around the lampposts. The third grade classroom boasted the children's handiwork of paper icicles, snowmen, and cut out wreaths and trees pasted on the windows.

Since Toddy had never known a real Christmas, Helene enjoyed planning lots of surprises. Olivia had Mr. Ferrin cut a tall evergreen on the property and bring it into the parlor for the girls to decorate. They spent days making circles of gilt paper chains and strings of cranberries and popcorn to drape on the tree. The ornaments Olivia had ordered from a mail-order catalog arrived in plenty of time to hang on the tree too.

For Toddy, Christmas Eve was the most special time of all. When Mrs. Hale and the girls arrived back home after the church program, the spicy scent of the tall cedar filled the parlor with its fragrance, the sweeping branches of the tree were ablaze with the light of dozens of candles. When her eyes saw the mound of packages tucked around the base of the tree, Toddy's mouth fell open.

"Go on, Toddy. Don't you want to open your presents?" Helene urged.

Toddy opened one after another. There were wonderful books, games, and pretty things to wear. Finally, she reached for a big box pushed way under the lower boughs. After tearing off the colorful wrapping, she took off the lid.

Within was a large china doll, its painted face framed by long dark curls. It was exquisitely dressed in a green velvet coat trimmed with lace and tiny white kid buttoned shoes.

As she lifted it out, the doll's blue eyes opened and looked directly into Toddy's. Toddy felt a little dart jab her heart. A painful memory flashed into her mind. Greystone, Miss Clinock's office, her mother saying good-bye. "I'll bring you back a big French doll. You'd like that, wouldn't you?" The promise made and broken. The emptiness of being deserted . . .

Ever so carefully, Toddy placed the doll back in its box. After Christmas it remained stiffly propped against the pillows of the window seat in her room. She never played with it.

11

"Grandmother, I want to give Toddy a birthday party," Helene began. "Since she's been here, she's never had a real one. And she'll be thirteen this year."

May sunshine flowed in through the windows of the dining room where Olivia and Helene were having breakfast alone. Toddy had already left for school.

"I'd like it to be a surprise party. We could keep everything secret until the last minute. I'm sure Kit and Laurel will help. What do you think?"

Mrs. Hale carefully buttered her toast before replying. Could it actually be *five* years since Toddy had come to live with them? Why, she was already in the eighth grade. Good heavens, how quickly the time had passed. Olivia shook her head at the thought.

Helene was watching her grandmother and took this as a refusal. Disappointment covered her thin face. "I promise I won't overdo, and Clara will help me. Won't you change your mind? Please?"

"Change my mind?" Mrs. Hale exclaimed. A hint of a smile softened her expression as she realized what Helene was thinking. "No! Indeed I won't! I think giving Toddy a party is a splendid idea."

Helene had already planned the party in her mind, and she quickly enlisted the help of both Clara and

Thomas. It would be a luncheon served in the garden, for the early June weather was sure to be pleasant. There would be chicken salad and tiny sandwiches, a fruit mold, lemonade, and of course, Toddy's favorite cake, German chocolate.

Kit and Laurel quickly agreed to help keep everything a secret until the special day. Helene painted lovely watercolor invitations to send out to Toddy's friends. Finally the big day arrived.

At breakfast Helene asked, "Toddy, would you mind going downtown for me this morning? I want to finish my needlepoint, and I'm out of blue thread."

"Of course." Toddy agreed, as she always did with Helene. Helene gave her a long list of other errands, a list guaranteed to keep the birthday girl away from the house for at least two hours.

A short while later, Laurel showed up. Kit came not long after finishing her morning chores at the farm.

While Thomas blew up balloons and strung them around the gazebo, Laurel and Kit helped Clara set up the table and chairs. Next, Laurel smoothed the pink tablecloth as Kit placed a crystal vase of colorful fragrant roses from Mr. Ferrin's garden in the center of the table.

At her chair on the sun porch, Helene finished the handwritten place cards. She placed each card in a small porcelain flower holder as the party favor for each guest. Helene's face was flushed, and her grandmother glanced anxiously at her.

"Mrs. Hale, this may be too much," Clara fussed. "Planning a party is one thing, but giving it is another. Helene might need to go upstairs and rest."

Olivia felt concern too. But she certainly wasn't going to spoil the day for her granddaughter. "Let her enjoy herself, Clara," she said firmly. "Helene doesn't get many chances like this. If she has to stay in bed tomorrow, well, so be it."

Olivia hoped she wouldn't regret this decision. All her life, Helene had been forced to listen to gloomy predictions about her health: She couldn't do this, and she couldn't go there. Planning this party for Toddy had given her enormous pleasure. Olivia turned to walk back inside. She would let her fears go for now.

Everything went according to the plan. The guests arrived and hid in the garden. Clara watched for Toddy and then alerted everyone to quiet down. When Toddy came inside, Clara immediately took the packages and sent the birthday girl to the garden to see Helene.

"Surprise! Happy birthday!"

Mrs. Hale stood at the parlor window that overlooked the garden, watching the surprise. She smiled. The sound of girlish laughter reached her ears. A crowd of pastel-colored dresses had gathered around Toddy. What a good time the girls were going to have. Helene had been right. It was a wonderful idea to give Toddy a surprise party.

My, how the years have flown, she sighed. If Toddy was thirteen, then Helene was nearly eighteen. Olivia breathed a prayer of thanksgiving. Helene had not been expected to live this long. Her granddaughter had seemed happier and more alive ever since Toddy's arrival five years before. The two got along so well. The change at the Hale house had been a good one.

"Excuse me, madam." Clara's voice interrupted Olivia's thoughts. She turned to see her housekeeper standing in the doorway, a strange expression on her face.

"Yes, what is it, Clara?"

"There's—well, ma'am, there's a person at the front door who insists on seeing you."

"A person?" Olivia frowned. "What do you mean? What kind of person?"

Clara quickly looked back over her shoulder and started to say something, but before she could, a woman pushed her aside and strode into the parlor.

"Mrs. Hale?"

The first thing Olivia saw was a tall green plumed hat that looked as though it weighted down the visitor's head. Under its brim emerged a mass of orange curls. Olivia guessed the woman was in her early thirties, but the thick makeup and cheap clothing made it hard to tell.

The stranger carried a red parasol that she tapped as she set it down in front of her. "You are Mrs. Olivia Hale?" she repeated in an English accent.

"Yes," Olivia's voice was cool. She started to ask, "And *you* are . . ." but before she could, the woman placed both hands on the handle of the parasol, leaned forward, and announced, "I'm Mazel Todd, Mrs. Hale, and I've come for my daughter."

This startling announcement sent a chill racing through Olivia's body. She stared back at the woman. As she tried to absorb the shock, she let her gaze sweep from the quivering green feathers on the astonishing hat down to the pointed toes of the high-heeled boots. All the time her mind was racing. She had to gather her wits about her enough to realize what the woman had said and deal with this dreadful turn of events.

The two women locked eyes. Mazel blinked first and turned away. She shifted her feet, then twisted the long, sleazy silk gloves she was carrying.

"Is she here? My little girl. Where is she?"

"Won't you sit down, Mrs. Todd." Olivia gestured to one of the velvet armchairs near the marble fireplace.

With a swish of her skirt, Mazel perched on the edge of the chair, holding her beaded purse with one hand.

All of Olivia's instincts tensed for battle. This woman spelled trouble, of that she was sure. What kind she didn't know, but like an experienced soldier, she braced herself for combat. She waited for the woman to speak. Mazel's eyes were roaming around the room. Olivia was forced to open the conversation.

"May I inquire how you happen to come here, Mrs. Todd?" Olivia asked. "And, what is the purpose of your visit?"

"I told you already." The woman's voice was husky, and her fake accent had mysteriously vanished. "I come for my kid, that's what!"

"But Toddy lives here now. I adopted her, Mrs. Todd." Olivia tried to keep the tone of her voice even. "I signed papers from the Rescuers and Providers' Society, the organization that brought Toddy from Greystone Orphanage in Boston."

Mazel's face flushed. She reached into her purse to pull something out, which she popped into her mouth. "Them people had no right to do that!" The wet smacking of gum slurred her words. "I didn't give them no permission for her to be adopted!"

"Surely you understood that children left over six months are put up for adoption."

"I don't remember any such thing," Mazel snapped. "How did I know our troupe would get another engagement in England? We was billed as headliners in Germany and Austria. Why, we had posters in five different languages!"

"You've just returned from an engagement in Europe then?"

Mazel swept back one of the long plumes on her hat. She looked like a chicken showing off its feathers. "Well, no, not just. I mean, we got back, but we had to go on the road again and—"

Mazel began to shift uneasily. "Well, not right away. I mean, I assumed Toddy was safe and well took care of."

The woman pulled a lacey white handkerchief from her purse and began dabbing her eyes. "And then when I come to get my baby girl, they told me she was gone!"

"*Seven years later?*" Olivia could hardly believe what she was hearing.

Mazel lifted her chin, put her handkerchief away, and glared at Olivia. Olivia pressed on.

"I understand Toddy was only six when she was brought to Greystone. Didn't it occur to you she might be put up for placement? You had to have signed release forms when you left her there."

"I don't recall signin' no such thing!"

"But you did, Mrs. Todd. I have such a paper with your signature on it," Mrs. Hale replied, her emotions now under control.

"I don't believe you. Where?"

"In my safe-deposit box at the bank."

Mazel was now fidgeting with the chain on her purse, knotting and unknotting it.

"How did you find out where Toddy was?"

"I run into an old friend who knew about the Orphan Train. They keep records, you know."

"But Greystone is clear across the country, in Massachusetts. You mean you traveled all this way to get her?"

The rouge on the woman's cheeks deepened. "What do you mean?"

"Just what I asked. And where do you propose to take Toddy to live? Where will she go to school? She's very bright, you know. In another year, she'll start high school." Mrs. Hale's words were beginning to sharpen.

When Mazel didn't reply right away, Olivia kept on. "Why did you really come to Meadowridge, Mrs. Todd? It isn't exactly on the main road from Boston. I think somehow your profession brought you nearby, and somehow you found out where Toddy was." Olivia remembered seeing a recent newspaper ad about a dance troupe at the county fair in Minersville, the next town over.

"In fact, I think you had no intention whatsoever of seeing Toddy . . . until you learned who had adopted her and you saw this house."

Mazel's eyes widened. She looked startled, then a little frightened. Olivia knew she had called the woman's bluff.

"I think your curiosity brought you here, Mrs. Todd. And your greed. How much do you want?"

"Why, why—" Mazel jumped up from the chair. "That's insulting!"

"I believe it's true," Olivia declared quietly. "But I also feel that children should be with their natural parents whenever possible. And since you've come such a long way and gone to so much trouble, perhaps we should get Toddy and let her decide for herself. She's out in the garden with her friends." Olivia glanced out the parlor window overlooking the garden.

"You know, *of course,* what day this is?" Olivia's gaze did not waver.

Mazel's painted red lips twitched in a nervous smile. "Oh, sure, I come by the school and seen it was closed. It's the start of summer vacation."

Olivia swallowed the instant anger she felt at the thought this woman did not even remember the date of her child's birth. "Shall I call Toddy in now?"

Mazel threw the strap of her purse over her wrist. "Oh, I don't want to take her away from her friends. Goodness knows, the kid probably won't remember me anyway. It's been so long—" Her voice sounded shrill.

"So, Mrs. Todd, what do you propose to do now?"

"Well, I didn't mean to upset everybody." She shrugged and slowed down her loud smacking. "I don't really have a proper home for a kid. We're tourin' all over the state, you know, and the company don't pay for families. It wouldn't be no life for a kid—I mean, a young girl."

"It's up to you, Mrs. Todd. Do you want to take Toddy with you?"

At this point, the panic on Mazel's face was as dense as the makeup. She squirmed under Olivia's steely-eyed look. "I want to do what's best for her, you see."

"Then, let's agree on it." Olivia unclenched the hands she had been gripping together and walked over to her desk.

"If you will sign a written statement that you will not contact me or Toddy in any way again, I shall write a check to cover all your expenses in coming here."

Olivia slid a piece of her monogrammed stationery onto the blotter, picked up her pen, and dipped it in the inkwell. Her quick, firm handwriting quickly covered the page with a few strong, clear sentences. After Mazel had signed it, Olivia sat down and wrote out a check, folded it, and handed it to Mazel, who slipped it quickly into her purse.

"Good afternoon, Mrs. Todd." Rising and moving to the parlor door, Olivia held it open. "My housekeeper will see you out."

In the parlor, Olivia sank slowly into the sofa. She was trembling, and her heart was beating very fast. She was far too old for this kind of tension. What a brazen piece of work that woman was. Thank goodness she had been able to see through the trickery.

Olivia closed her eyes, drew a shaky hand across her brow, and took a deep breath.

A soft tap sounded at the door.

"I thought you could do with a spot of tea, ma'am," Clara said, placing a small tray on the table in front of her employer.

"Thank you, Clara." The two women exchanged a wordless glance. "I certainly can."

Later that afternoon, Mazel arrived back in Minersville just in time for the night's performance at the county fair.

"Did you see her?" Flo's voice crackled above the loud noices outside the small canvas tent as she fastened her sequined green costume.

"Yeh." Mazel cut her answer short.

"Well, is she doin' all right?" Flo arranged a wide band of bright feathers in her hair. Since she had never felt right about Mazel ditching the kid, she really wanted to know what had happened to Toddy.

"I tell you, she's fine." Mazel finished arranging her own headband and stood up. "Hooked up with some rich folks. Don't need to say no more."

With that, Mazel stretched aside the tent's flap and strolled outside. The show was about to begin.

The Class of 1900

The afternoon sun sent long shadows across the grass as the four tennis players finished their set and prepared to go home. Tying the strings on her racket cover, Toddy shook back her curly hair.

Beside her, Chris pulled a white, V-necked sweater over his dark head. On the other side of the court, Laurel and her friend Dan were talking in low tones.

"Coming, you two?" Toddy called out.

Dan picked up the rackets on the ground. "Coming!"

The foursome walked across the wide lawn in front of Meadowridge High.

"Has anyone done our final book report yet?" Toddy asked.

Chris moaned. "Don't mention it, Toddy. *Ivanhoe*. So dull."

"Dull?" echoed Laurel. "I thought it was wonderful. So romantic."

"Then maybe you can help me write the two-thousand-word theme on it." Chris looked hopeful.

"Chris, do your own work!" Toddy sounded indignant. "You can't expect everyone to rescue you."

"Rescue? You mean like a gallant knight rescuing a fair damsel from the tower of the wicked king?"

"No, I don't mean that! Not unless you consider yourself a damsel in distress!" Toddy liked to clown around with Chris. A handsome six feet, he had become a champion runner and the star of the high school basketball team. Toddy considered it her job to keep him from getting conceited. "I mean like royalty. The Prince of Hemlock Hill." She made a big sweeping bow. "What is your highness's pleasure? How can we serve you, O Prince?"

"*You* should talk! The queen of Shakespeare. Portia, my love," he mocked, "can you spare a pound of flesh?"

"Oh no, your honor, but the Crown Prince of the royal house of Blanchard can!" countered Toddy.

Dan and Laurel looked at one another. Chris was mimicking Toddy's wonderful performance in the high school play, *The Merchant of Venice*.

Although he knew she was teasing, Chris colored under his tan. Toddy realized she might have gone a little too far. Then, as he tried to snatch her hair ribbon, she dodged and started to run. Chris, a natural athlete, took off after her.

Small and light but very fast, Toddy whisked through the iron gate of Hale House. Breathless, she leaned over the gate as he came panting up on the other side. They had left Laurel and Dan far below.

"Tortoise!" she teased.

"Don't you ever let up?" he scowled.

"Not when you're such an easy target."

A worried expression wrinkled his brow. "Toddy, you don't *really* think I'm—well, what you said, do you?"

She angled her head to one side, studying her friend intently. "Well, only a little—" The dimples on either side of her rosy mouth winked. "You know you wouldn't object if Laurel, or better still, Kit, wrote the book report for you. After all, she's the writer in the class, and you'd get a good grade. That'd make you feel like a king."

"That's not what I'm talking about."

"I don't remember what I said then."

"You do too," Chris insisted. "You know the part I mean, about my being the Prince of Hemlock Hill."

"Oh, that."

"Yes, that!"

"I must have hit a nerve if you're so upset about it," Toddy taunted.

"Come on, Toddy."

"Well, it's partially true. You know it is. All the girls admire you at school. Your father's the president of Meadowridge Bank, and your mother spoils you silly."

Chris knew there was some truth to this. As the two walked up the path to the house, he decided to change the subject. "Did I tell you my father is taking me up to the university the week after graduation? There's some kind of alumni weekend."

"Oh, you'll get in, Chris, no question." Although she didn't say so, Toddy felt sure Mr. Blanchard would make sure his son was accepted. The banker would either make a large donation to the building fund or maybe build a gymnasium.

"I don't know how I feel about going to the university when it comes right down to it," Chris admitted. "For one thing, I don't like the idea of going so far from Meadow-ridge. I mean—"

Chris stopped in mid-sentence. Looking at Toddy, he suddenly realized how pretty she was. In the slant of the setting sun, her red-gold hair flamed to life. Her neat figure fairly burst with energy. But it was Toddy's eyes that held him. They sparkled, hinting of mischief. Funny, he had never noticed them like this before.

"What's the matter?" Toddy prodded. "Are you afraid of being homesick?"

"No, it's not that," Chris jolted back into reality. "It's just that it'll be a long way to come—I mean, I'll miss seeing you, Toddy."

Toddy seemed amused. "Don't they let you out for holidays and good behavior?"

"Doggone it, Toddy, aren't you ever serious?" Chris was about to lose his temper. He leaned over the gate and yanked off her hair ribbon. She grabbed for it but missed.

"So long! See you at the picnic tomorrow!" he called over his shoulder, wrapping the ribbon around his fingers and trotting down the street toward Hemlock Hill.

"And don't be late!"

"I'll get you for this, Chris Blanchard! See if I don't!"

The small class of seniors had grown close during their four years together at Meadowridge High. During the class picnic there was lots of laughter, good-natured teasing, and jokes. The feast did not end with fried chicken and potato salad. The group enjoyed homemade pies and cakes and juicy watermelon.

After they had finished eating, Chris suggested to Toddy that they walk along the winding path down to the river below the meadow. To her annoyance, Chris continued an argument that had been interrupted by lunch.

"But I don't see why I can't take you to the awards banquet, Toddy."

"I've already told you, Chris. Helene and Mrs. Hale are coming. I'll be with them."

"But the seniors are going to have their own table. Don't they know you'll be sitting with your class?"

"Of course, they know that, Chris. And I can sit with you then. But Helene is so excited about the graduation, and I want her to feel a part of what I'm doing."

Toddy bunched up her blue-checked skirt to slide over a big rock. Chris slid down right behind her.

"But being with your class is important. It'll be the last time we'll all be together. Can't Helene understand that?"

"How could she, Chris?" Toddy stopped long enough to tighten the dark blue ribbon holding back her hair. Then she hopped to a ledge near the river, picked up a small rock, and skimmed it across the calm water. "Helene's never had a chance to go to a real school or be part of a real class. I'm just trying to give her the feeling of graduating. It means so much to her. Don't you see?"

Chris sighed and picked up another stone to toss. "Well, what about afterward? You know Mother wants to give our class a party after the banquet. You can go with me, can't you?"

"I don't know, Chris. I'm not sure."

Even though his rock landed on the far side, a scowl on Chris's face gave away his true feelings.

"What do you mean 'not sure'?" he demanded. "I told you about this party weeks ago. There won't be any party if you're not there. Why would I even want one if you aren't coming!" Chris didn't stop there. "It was Mother's idea anyway. I'll just call it off."

"You can't do that, Chris. Your mother would be upset and mad at me for being the cause."

They started walking again and reached the edge of the river.

"Then promise you'll work it out with Mrs. Hale and Helene," Chris finally said stubbornly.

"I think they're planning a surprise, Chris. I can't ruin it for them."

Chris wanted to make her agree, but he couldn't stay mad at her. In fact, he never stayed mad at her very long. Toddy was smiling at him right now. He found that irresistible.

Then, Toddy abruptly changed direction. As she hopped from rock to rock, Chris followed.

Toddy's footing wobbled on a slippery stone. "Whoops!" she cried.

Chris reached out, putting both his hands around her waist to steady her. He held her until she regained her footing.

"I'm all right, now. You can let go," she told him.

Chris's hands remained a split second longer, then he released her. She ran ahead with a few light steps. Making it to a strip of sand, she turned and waited until he came alongside her.

There's something different about Chris today, Toddy thought. Wonder what it is? He looked the same—tall and tan, clear blue eyes, with that lopsided grin. Her heart gave a strange little flutter.

What was coming over her? She had known Chris forever, or at least since she had come to live in Meadowridge nearly ten years ago. He was the first person her own age she had met. She still recalled that fun afternoon in Mr. Traherne's apple trees. Except for Kit and Laurel, Toddy felt Chris was her best friend. So why this new unsettling feeling?

She and Chris walked slowly now along the riverbank under the graceful swaying branches of the willows. There seemed to be an almost sleepy haze over everything. The afternoon sunlight dappled the water, making it glitter as it swirled into the eddies.

How many times had they walked together like this? Yet this day had a different quality, as though it were detached somehow from all the rest of the days they had ever been together. They weren't even teasing each other right now.

Chris took Toddy's hand in his. As if startled by the touch, they stopped. Toddy looked into his shining blue eyes but didn't say a word. She didn't want to spoil this special moment. Feeling a gathering tension she could not explain, Toddy withdrew her hand from his and took a few steps toward a cluster of wildflowers.

"I think I'll pick some of these for Helene," Toddy said, gathering some lupine and Queen Anne's lace into a small bouquet.

"Wildflowers don't last very long," Chris said.

Neither do days like this, Toddy thought, feeling a sweet kind of sadness knowing the lovely afternoon was nearly over.

Chris reached for her hand again, but both were now filled with flowers.

13

On the night of the awards banquet, the high school gymnasium had been turned into a banquet hall. Tables were set up all around the room. A special T-shaped one in the middle was reserved for such people as the principal and the mayor. The senior class table was draped with twisted streamers of green and gold crepe paper and decorated with great bunches of yellow daffodils centered in wreaths of green leaves and tall gold candles. Marking each senior's place was a rosette of gold and green satin ribbon with CLASS OF 1900 in sparkly gold letters to pin on a coat lapel or the shoulder of a dress.

Toddy waved to Kit and Laurel as she escorted Helene and Mrs. Hale to one of the tables reserved for the families of the graduates. Mrs. Hale looked regal in black lace and pearls, while Helene's lovely apricot dress gave color to her pale face.

"I wish I could sit with you, but the seniors all have to be together," she told Helene as she seated them with the parents of her classmates.

"Of course, Toddy, I understand. You go on and be with your friends," she reassured her. "Grandmother and I will be fine."

Toddy looked back over her shoulder toward Helene. Once again she wondered if all the fuss over Helene's heart condition didn't make her too conscious of it. Was Helene really that fragile? Toddy wished she could get Helene out of the house more, but Helene's health kept her isolated most of the time. Toddy tried to help by inviting friends over, and Helene always seemed to enjoy them, but was this enough?

When Toddy reached the senior table, her troubling thoughts disappeared. Chris gave a soft admiring whistle. She had to admit she did feel pretty in her new white muslin dress with its embroidered daisies and wide green sash. She quickly sat down next to him, with Laurel and Kit sitting opposite.

After the dinner, the principal rose, tapped on his water glass with his fork, and waited for the hum of conversation to die down.

"Ladies and gentlemen, parents and friends, the Class of 1900!" Mr. Henson smiled with pride.

"Before we begin our ceremony, we have a treat in store. Many of you have heard this wonderful young lady in the church choir and on other special occasions. Tonight, she's going to sing for us. Miss Laurel Woodward."

Laurel's voice rose sweetly, each note clear and true. When she finished, the room was hushed. Then slowly the clapping began and went on and on, even after Laurel had returned to her place at the table.

At last, Mr. Henson announced, "And now our first award. For his outstanding athletic ability in both track and basketball, as the winner of four letters and the trophy for the county Athlete of the Year, our own Chris Blanchard."

Toddy joined in the wild clapping as Chris received the engraved cup. Then her heart swelled with pride when Kit, the writer among them, received the award for English Composition. But when her own name was announced for the best dramatic performance of the year, Toddy could hardly believe her ears.

She had loved playing the role of Portia in Shakespeare's *Merchant of Venice*. Even before winning a part, she had volunteered to paint scenery for different plays, sell advertising for the programs, help with costumes, or usher on opening nights. She enjoyed being involved in the theater.

Yet, Miss Tuttle's words that day were still etched in stone in Toddy's heart. Toddy still struggled with the feeling there was something shameful about it, that she was nothing more than "a theater brat."

As she was handed the engraved plaque, however, these feelings momentarily faded. People were applauding her. Mrs. Hale and Helene were clapping too. She was being rewarded for doing something she really loved to do.

Olivia listened as Toddy accepted the award. She remembered Toddy's moving performance that night. Toddy was growing up right in front of her eyes. Here she was, her red-gold curls swirled up on her head, giving an acceptance speech. Was Toddy a born actress? Would she leave someday and follow her parents' footsteps? Was it right for Olivia to expect Toddy to remain with Helene forever? What would happen if she left?

Olivia watched Helene's thin hands clap in delight. Her granddaughter was so delicate. In the room's dim light, she looked even more fragile. Olivia nervously pleated the napkin in her own lap. She was frightened.

As Toddy sat down, Chris wrapped his arm around her and gave her a tight squeeze. It was an act that didn't go unnoticed.

Bernice Blanchard, who sat at the next table, narrowed her eyes and gritted her teeth. Why had her dear boy—such a catch—set his eyes on this little nobody from nowhere? He could have any girl in town. He received a steady stream of invitations to parties and outings from daughters of some of the best families in Meadowridge. Not that Olivia Hale wasn't considered the top of Meadowridge society. Now, if it had been Olivia's granddaughter, that would be a different story. But poor Helene! Thank goodness Chris would be going away to the university in the fall. Surely, time and distance would stop his foolish infatuation with Toddy. Bernice watched them together and felt more and more irritated.

Graduation day, Toddy was standing in front of her mirror putting the finishing touches on her hair when Helene tapped on her bedroom door.

"Need any help?" she asked.

Bright June sunlight poured in through the open windows of Toddy's bedroom. As Helene stepped in, a breeze sent the ruffled curtains billowing like sails.

"Oh yes, Helene, the buttons on my right cuff. I can't manage them with my left hand. Or maybe I'm just too nervous."

"*You* nervous? The one who won the best actress award? Nothing to be nervous about. All you have to do is go up when they call your name and get your diploma."

"That's just it. I can play Portia or somebody else." Toddy held her hand out for Helene to fasten the tiny pearl buttons. "But I'm not so sure when it comes to myself."

"You'll do fine, don't worry. And Grandmother and I will be there to give you moral support and clap our hands off when you stand up.

"There, you look lovely. The dress is perfect."

Toddy twirled around, sending her white dotted swiss skirt flaring.

Just then, another tap sounded at the bedroom door, and Mrs. Hale pushed it open. She carried a tiny package with a silver ribbon.

"Are you nearly ready, Toddy? I thought the graduates were supposed to be at school a half hour before the program starts."

"Yes, ma'am," Toddy replied, remembering all the times she'd been late to things in the past.

"Maybe this will help," Olivia offered her the daintily wrapped package.

Toddy looked at her in surprise.

"Well, go ahead, Toddy, open it!" Helene urged.

Toddy pulled the ribbons to reveal a tiny leather box. Lifting its lid she saw an exquisite gold oval watch suspended from a delicate chain.

"Do you like it?" Helene asked. "Here, let me put it on for you."

"Oh, it's beautiful! Thank you! Thank you so much!"

"The jeweler set it for you, Toddy. So there's no excuse for you to be late to your own graduation, or anything else in the future!" said Mrs. Hale with a twinkle in her eye.

Toddy hugged Helene. "I know you picked this out for me. It's the nicest thing I've ever had. Thank you!"

"Oh, Toddy, I love you! What would we ever do without you?"

An hour later Olivia Hale sat in one of the rows reserved for the parents and family of the graduates. Helene sat beside her.

"Zephronia Victorine Todd" was known as Toddy Hale, but her birth name would be written in fine calligraphy on her diploma. Suddenly, Olivia had a disturbing thought. The memory of that dreadful day on Toddy's thirteenth birthday played itself in her mind as frequently as a phonograph. She thought about it again today. Although she felt guilty about never having told Toddy about her mother's visit, Olivia knew some things were better left unsaid. After all, at eighteen Toddy had her whole life in front of her.

And then there was Helene. Olivia glanced at her granddaughter sitting happily beside her. The chiseled profile seemed even sharper. Had she lost more weight? Olivia felt a little stirring of alarm, and she moved uneasily in her seat.

Olivia had already suggested to Helene that the three of them go somewhere this summer. It could be a pleasant change of climate and scenery for Helene and a graduation present for Toddy too.

Yes, that would still be the wise thing to do. Close the house and go. Then if that woman got any ideas about coming back into Toddy's life after graduation, they would be far away.

Olivia thought Europe was the right choice. It would be educational for both the girls. She wanted to consult some European doctors about Helene too, so they could make it a leisurely journey, no hurrying from country to country. Why, there was no reason to hurry. They could take months traveling, even a year—

But Helene had said no, at least not this summer. "Toddy wouldn't say this, Grandmother, but I'm sure she'd rather spend this summer at home. This'll be the last summer with many of her friends."

Olivia settled down as the graduation ceremony began. Yes, she could postpone her plans for a while. Helene was right. However, she would keep the idea of Europe packed on the shelf of her mind until the right time did come along.

14

Weeks of sunny days brought picnics and tennis, bicycling out to the river, afternoons of croquet or badminton on someone's lawn, and sipping lemonade under shady trees. The soft summer evenings offered twilight band concerts in the park, gathering on porches or in parlors singing around a piano, ice cream socials at the community hall, and strolling home after the Sunday youth meeting at church. It flew by like migrating birds across Arkansas.

On the first Sunday morning in August, Reverend Brewster made a special announcement.

"Come to receive a blessing," Reverend Brewster told them from the pulpit in front of the Meadowridge Church. "Pastor Matthew Scott will visit us again after all these years. The revival will begin on Wednesday and will continue each evening for the rest of the week. Don't let anything keep you from these divine appointments."

Chris was waiting outside the church for Toddy. He took off his brown leather cap and bowed slightly when she arrived.

"Wouldn't you know it would be the same week as the carnival?" he complained as they walked down the stone steps.

Toddy looked shocked. "Shame on you, Chris Blanchard. Didn't you hear anything Reverend Brewster said? Not to let anything keep you from attending?"

Chris tried to look chastened. "Then *you're* planning to go?"

"Of course."

Chris hesitated a moment absorbing this information, then said, "I just wanted to see if you'd go to the carnival with me. It opens tomorrow. They're already setting up over at the town park."

Toddy and Chris were approaching the Hale's open carriage where Mrs. Hale and Helene were waiting. Toddy slowed, glancing at them.

"All right, Chris Blanchard. I'll go with you, but only if Mrs. Hale says I may. But if I do, you have to promise to come to the revival meetings."

The following evening, Toddy poked her head in the door of Helene's room. "I'll tell you all about the carnival when I get home, Helene!"

Helene was propped up in bed reading a book. Through the light of the lamp's glass shade, Toddy saw the smile. "Have fun, Toddy. I'll see you later."

With a wave of her hand, Toddy flew down the stairs to where Chris was talking with Mrs. Hale. Toddy instantly noticed how handsome he looked in his white trousers and long-sleeved blue pinstriped shirt. She was glad she had chosen this white cotton dress for the occasion.

"Have a good time, you two," Olivia called out as they went out the front door.

Over the tops of the trees they could see lights from the carnival lighting up the lavender evening sky. The tinny sound of calliope music from the merry-go-round swirled through the Meadowridge air and up the hill, calling them with its own distinctive charm.

A strange little tingle quivered through Toddy. When Chris tucked her hand through his arm, she wondered what the strange feeling was.

The smell of canvas and sawdust mingled with the strong odors of the horses tethered near the tents. Barkers from the concession booths yelled "take a chance" and "try your luck" at the couple as they walked by.

The sticky sweetness of cotton candy melted into the rich greasy aroma of popcorn. Chris held Toddy's hand as they meandered down the midway.

"Win your sweetheart a prize, mister!" one seller cried out hoarsely.

Chris decided to give the game a try. Much to the man's dismay, Chris hit the target dead center each time.

"Try another round, why don't you, sonny?" the man pleaded before handing them their prize.

Toddy pulled Chris away, laughing and carrying the prize, a painted plaster bulldog.

"Let's ride the Ferris wheel," Chris suggested.

A calloused hand took their strip of tickets. A smoking cigarette dangled from one end of the operator's mouth. He raised the safety bar, and Toddy and Chris settled themselves in the flimsy seat. A minute later they were suddenly thrust swiftly back and upward into the night sky.

"Oh!" Toddy cried as Chris put his arm protectively around the back ledge of the seat.

At the top, the Ferris wheel stopped with a jolt.

"Oh, my!" Toddy giggled nervously.

Below them the lamps along Main Street looked like twinkling pins in a piece of black felt.

"Scared?" Chris teased, purposely rocking their chair.

"Chris, don't!" she cried, clutching his arm.

"Don't worry. You're perfectly safe . . . with me." His arm dropped down on her shoulder and he leaned a little closer.

"Toddy," Chris's voice was wavering like the swinging seat. "Would you wear my class pin if I gave it to you before I leave for the university?"

Her heart jumped. She felt light-headed.

"I don't know if that's a good idea, Chris," she replied at last. "You're going to be meeting lots of girls at college."

"Please, Toddy, I want you to have it. Going away isn't going to make any difference to me." The gentle wind almost carried away his words. "You know I love you, don't you?"

Just then the Ferris wheel started again with a jerk, and they were whirled down and around again. After another quick spin, they came to an abrupt stop and the ride was over.

"Think about it, won't you, Toddy?" Chris's blue eyes pleaded as they got out.

A short while later, the couple passed a large striped tent along the midway.

"Come one, come all, ladies and gentlemen!" a thin man with a mustache hollered at the passersby. "See the Toast of Paree, the beautiful, stupendous Trenton Threesome." The man tapped his long walking stick on the dirt and squared the shoulders of his yellow and green plaid suit. "Why, these ladies have danced before the crowned heads of Europe! Just fifty cents a head, folks. Step right up!" With that, he touched the brim of his derby hat. "Get your tickets right here."

At that moment, three women pranced onto a narrow stage. They were dressed in matching orange, red, and bright blue costumes. The colorful plumes of their hats bounced with each step, and the flounces of their fringed skirts whirled to the blaring music from the brass funnel of a gramophone inside the tent.

As Toddy watched them, an icy finger trailed down her spine. Rooted to the spot, her eyes were fixed on the painted faces of the three dancers. The sounds of their high-heeled boots tapping across the stage made her stomach turn.

Toddy loosened her hand from Chris's, turned and walked quickly toward a nearby exit.

"Hey, Toddy, wait up!"

She could hear Chris's voice right behind her.

"What's the matter?"

The hot, choking sensation gripping her throat made it hard to draw a breath. "I've had enough, Chris," she replied. "I want to go home now."

"Well, sure." A puzzled Chris fell into step beside her.

As they walked back along the quiet, residential streets and up the hill, the music of the carnival slowly faded into the distance. At the Hale's gate, they halted.

"Was it anything I said, Toddy?"

She could see the anxious expression on his face.

Toddy shook her head. "No, I'm just tired, I guess."

"You *did* have a good time though, didn't you?"

"Oh yes, Chris. Thanks for taking me."

As she turned to push open the gate, Chris caught her arm. "And you'll think about what I asked you, won't you?"

"Yes, Chris, I will."

Chris leaned forward to help her with the gate. "I do love you, Toddy." His voice sounded husky now.

"I know," she answered softly. "Good night, Chris."

He stood there watching her slim figure in the white dress disappear on the dark veranda and through the lighted front door. Placing his hands in his pockets, he turned to walk back down the hill toward home.

On the other side of the door, Toddy stood for a minute trying to compose herself before going up to Helene's room.

What had come over her at that dancers' booth? It was as though she had suddenly been jerked backward in time. For a moment she had been terrified, afraid that she was being sucked into a great big hole.

An involuntary shudder swept over her. Toddy shook her head as if to clear it. The memories! Oh, the memories. Dancers tapping with high-heeled shoes on a stage. The paint and feathers. The colorful costumes. Her mother . . . Flo . . . long ago.

As she leaned back against the front door, Toddy took in a big breath to calm herself. For that split second she had felt like the carnival was more real than her life with the Hales. Somehow the life she had once known was still living in the deep recesses of her heart, even at eighteen.

"Is that you, Toddy?"

Mrs. Hale's question interrupted her thought, propelling her back into the present.

"Helene's waiting up for you. Why don't you stop and see her?"

"Yes, ma'am, I'm going," Toddy replied.

15

Leaning back on the pale pink pillows, Helene eagerly listened to everything Toddy had to say about the carnival. Curled up on the end of the high brass bed, Toddy tried to make it as vivid as she could. Helene would never have the chance to experience it herself, so Toddy loved to dramatize as much as possible. Tonight, she imitated the rowdy bark of the man at the shooting gallery. Helene laughed appreciatively at Toddy's antics.

Winding up her recital, Toddy noticed the book on Helene's marble-topped bedside table and asked, "What are you reading now?"

Helene picked it up and showed her the title *The Lady with the Lamp*. "It's about Florence Nightingale. She was a nurse who saved hundreds of wounded soldiers' lives during the Crimean War. She always held her lamp up high as she made her rounds among the soldiers' cots at night. The men welcomed the sight of her shadow and gave her that name."

"Saved lives? How?"

"She applied things she had learned at a German nursing school. Simple things like cleanliness. Things no one had thought of before." Helene handed the book to Toddy. "And she heard God speaking to her, telling her what to do."

Toddy sat up straight.

"You mean she *actually* heard God's voice? What did it sound like?"

Toddy's excitement showed.

"Well, the book says it wasn't like regular talking. She heard it as an inner knowing. It directed her to do things no one had ever done. It showed her how to take care of the wounded and dying. Would you like to read it?"

An hour later, Toddy was still awake reading. When she finally blew out her lamp, Toddy could not go to sleep right away.

How wonderful to be able to help sick people, Toddy thought. And to know that God had called you to do just that.

Florence Nightingale had started schools in England to train young women to become nurses. Now there were schools in the United States patterned on her ideas. Toddy wondered if Miss Tuttle, her old enemy, had trained in such a school. Probably not. Miss Tuttle wasn't anything like the Lady with the Lamp.

Toddy scrunched up her pillow to make it more comfortable. What a worthwhile way to spend your life.

She was drifting off when all of a sudden, out of nowhere, another thought struck her: What if you become a nurse, Toddy?

Toddy's eyes opened wide into the blackness of her bedroom. Would it be possible? Once in a while she had entertained the thought of the theater, but she knew that wasn't realistic, even though she enjoyed drama. But nursing!

Toddy's mind shifted into racing speed. She had always loved taking care of Helene. Helene needed her so. How many times had she brought her medicine and placed cool cloths on her aching head? How often had she been there to sit through one of Helene's many spells?

It felt good to be needed. Toddy needed to be needed. And nurses were people who were needed!

The idea now had a momentum all its own. Toddy decided she would talk to Mrs. Hale and pray about it too. Maybe God would tell her what to do, just as he had Florence Nightingale.

On Wednesday night, Toddy met Laurel outside the church. Kit arrived a few minutes later with Miss Cady, their elementary school teacher. Kit was now living in town with Miss Cady, who was trying to help her get a scholarship to go on to college.

Before going in, Toddy glanced around for Chris. She didn't see him.

Toddy had never heard Pastor Scott preach before, but she remembered him well. His voice had the same husky sound as it had on the Orphan Train, but the hair around his temples was grayer than she remembered. Dressed in a simple green-checked cotton dress, Anna Scott sat in the front pew. Toddy's heart warmed to see her again. She determined to say hello after the service.

At the end of the night as everyone flowed out of the church, Toddy, Laurel, and Kit remained behind.

"Mrs. Scott!" Toddy exclaimed, rushing up toward the front.

Anna Scott's heart warmed. Although it had been over a decade, she could recognize her "Three Musketeers" anywhere.

"Toddy, is that you? How beautiful you are! And Laurel and Kit!"

Anna blinked back the tears. She embraced the girls, holding each one gently for a few seconds.

"I'm so glad to see you at last. It's been such a long time."

At last, the foursome sat down on the front pew. Matthew Scott was talking with some men in the front of the church.

"It looks like we have some time," Anna started, the fine wrinkles around her mouth moving when she spoke.

Her hair was swept up in a tight bun, and Toddy noticed gray streaks throughout. She still remembered the time the three of them had told Mrs. Scott their secret.

"Toddy, Mrs. Hale has written me faithfully about you," Anna began, taking Toddy's hand in her own. "I was so delighted to hear about your drama award. You are a talented young lady.

"And Kit, your writing," Anna went on. "I know the good Lord is going to open doors for you. He has a way of doing that, you know."

Kit smiled. "Yes, ma'am, I'm hoping so."

"Laurel, are you going to continue your singing?"

"I don't know, Mrs. Scott," Laurel's voice sounded uncertain. Laurel's dark eyes avoided hers. It was probably best not to pursue this right now, she decided.

Just then, Matthew Scott, in a shabby suitcoat and flowing tie, approached, looking very much like Toddy remembered him. He was carrying a Bible with a worn black cover and yellowed pages.

"Hello, girls," he greeted them. "It is so good to see what God is doing here in Meadowridge. I hope you'll come back the rest of the week."

The three girls left with promises to return.

On Friday night, the evangelist took his place in the pulpit. After the opening prayer, he held up some torn pieces of paper.

"Friends, tonight I'm throwing away my prepared notes. I feel led of the Holy Spirit to speak from my heart."

The church was so still that no one seemed to be breathing. Matthew Scott leafed through his Bible.

" 'What is that in thine hand?' the Lord asked Moses. Moses looked down and replied, 'A rod.' " Pastor Scott was reading from Exodus 4, verse 2.

"To Moses, it was a simple ordinary shepherd's stick. It had little value and certainly no power. It wasn't even a sword or a weapon Moses could use to force Pharaoh to release the Hebrew people from their bondage in Egypt."

Toddy sat quietly in her pew listening with everyone else.

"But with God's almighty power, that rod became the miraculous instrument that parted the Red Sea!"

Toddy could see Pastor Scott's eyes roving the congregation. For some reason, she swallowed hard.

"Aren't we like Moses?" he went on. "Don't we look at what we have in our hands and wonder what we can do with it?" He paused. "Friends, each of us has very precious gifts. Like Moses's rod, they may seem small or commonplace, but dedicated to God's will, they can change our lives and the lives of those around us."

His words reached far beyond Toddy's ears and mind, penetrating into her soul.

Pastor Scott continued. "Power often lies hidden in the obvious. Tonight, I want you to look at your rod, at the gifts and talents God has given you. Tonight, we're going to ask God to show you exactly what he wants you to do."

When he finished, there was a hush. His sermon seemed to have had a profound effect on his listeners. No one moved or stirred until the organist struck the first few chords of the closing hymn.

Slowly the congregation began to file out of the pews. Unlike previous nights, tonight no one was talking. Even Toddy, Laurel, and Kit weren't saying a word. As she left, Toddy noticed a group of young men in the back of the church quickly leaving.

"Can I walk you home?"

It was Chris. He was waiting on the church steps a short distance apart from the other young men who had just left.

"Not tonight, Chris. Kit and I are spending the night at Laurel's." Toddy waited a few moments for her two friends to catch up. "Besides, I didn't think you were coming."

"I came," he replied, disappointed in her answer. "Oh, well, see you tomorrow."

As the strains of the last hymn floated on the summer air, the three girls linked arms and walked down the rest of the steps. The soft chirping of crickets merged with the low whinny of the horses tied to the nearby fence.

The evening air was fresh, cool, delicately scented with the fragrance from all the summer gardens they passed. The trio marched forward, together, the bond of friendship and love strong between them.

Coming through the Woodwards' gate, Toddy felt a surge of faith well up within her. She felt light and carefree. The memories of the past and concerns about the future seemed to evaporate. It no longer mattered. She was in God's hands, and he would take care of her. Like Moses, the Lord would show her the special rod he had given her. And she would learn how to use it.

16

Olivia looked up from the evening paper to see Toddy standing in the doorway of the parlor.

"Oh, yes, the Blanchard dinner party, isn't it?"

"Yes, ma'am," she replied. "New Year's Eve."

With her gold-red hair swept up, Toddy looked amazingly grown-up and pretty, Olivia thought. The little pixie had become a real beauty. No wonder the Blanchard boy was still smitten even after having been at the university these past three months.

"You look very nice, Toddy," she said.

Toddy's eyes danced. Lifting her skirt gracefully, she made a slow pirouette. The dress had a royal blue velvet bodice, puffed sleeves, and a graceful skirt.

"This is such a beautiful dress, Mrs. Hale. Thank you so much." Toddy stopped twirling and lowered her voice. "But I must admit, I'm a little terrified. All of Chris's relatives will be there."

A smile tugged at Olivia's mouth. She motioned to Toddy to come closer. Toddy walked over and stood by her armchair.

"Don't let Bernice Blanchard intimidate you, Toddy," Olivia said. "She'll try, you know. You're charming and considerate. Just be yourself."

Just then the sound of the front doorbell being twisted echoed through the downstairs.

"Toddy, was Helene feeling all right when you came down?"

Toddy's smile faded. "She said she was better, that she was going to read for a while." Toddy hesitated. "Do you think I should stay?"

"No, of course not, child. Helene would be upset if she thought you were missing a party on her account. I'm sure Clara and I can keep an eye on things."

"Toddy, Mr. Chris Blanchard is here to pick you up," Clara said as she stuck her head in the parlor.

"Evening, Mrs. Hale."

Chris stepped into the room looking especially formal in his dark blue suit and white ruffled shirt.

"Good evening, Chris. Have you enjoyed your holidays?"

"Yes, thank you, ma'am."

Chris could not keep his eyes off Toddy. The deep blue of her dress set off her gorgeous red hair.

"I suppose you've been busy with sports?" Mrs. Hale's question brought him back.

"Well, yes, ma'am," he flustered, "as a matter of fact—"

"And when do you have to return to the university?"

Chris looked gloomy.

"Day after tomorrow, I'm afraid."

None too soon, Olivia thought, seeing how the two were gazing at each other.

Chris shifted uneasily. "I guess we better be going. Mother said dinner is going to be served promptly at seven."

"Yes, indeed, you'd best be off then."

"Happy New Year, Mrs. Hale," Chris politely added as he helped Toddy put on her evening cape.

"Yes, and the same to you and your family."

After they left, Olivia felt frustrated. First of all, she wasn't sure about this budding romance between Chris and Toddy. She had hoped to be away from Meadowridge by the holidays anyway; this would have solved the problem. The girls' wardrobes had been assembled, and their passports had already arrived. She had even purchased their tickets. But Helene had had a bad spell, and Dr. Woodward had advised against traveling. Olivia gave the newspaper a sharp snap and tried to keep her mind on the column she had been reading.

Their boots crunched the packed snow and their breath sent frosty plumes into the dark as Chris and Toddy walked. Before they went up the steps of the Blanchards' porch, Chris pulled Toddy gently back. Tilting her chin with one hand, he put the other into his coat pocket and pulled out a spray of mistletoe.

"See? I'm always prepared," he said mischievously, holding it over her head. "An early happy New Year, Toddy!" He leaned down and kissed her.

"Happy New Year, Chris," she whispered.

"I'm glad you're still wearing my pin," he said softly. And I want you to know I'm thinking about not going back to the university."

"What?" Toddy cried in alarm. She drew back and looked up at him. "If you don't go back, Chris, your parents will blame me."

Just then the front door opened and a beam of light enveloped them.

"Well, for heaven's sake, there you are!" Mrs. Blanchard exclaimed. "We were wondering what was keeping you. Come in. It's freezing out there. Hurry up. Don't let the cold air into the house." Her voice sounded annoyed.

Chris squeezed Toddy's hand, and they hurried up the steps and into the house.

The front staircase was decorated with boughs of evergreens looped with shiny red ribbons. The air was

111

fragrant with the scent of pine. Candles lit each of the big windows.

Chris helped Toddy off with her cape. As she took off the boots she'd worn to protect her pumps, she admired the eight-foot-tall cedar tree at the foot of the stairs. Garlands glittered in the light from dozens of tiny candles. Glistening balls reflected their sparkle while brightly painted tin birds nested in the sweeping branches.

"I'll go put these in the cloak room and be right back." Chris disappeared, leaving her alone with his mother.

Toddy's stomach tightened.

"Everything looks lovely, Mrs. Blanchard," she remarked politely.

"Thank you, Toddy. Everyone says I do have a certain talent for making things look attractive."

Mrs. Blanchard was regarding her in a way that made Toddy uncomfortable.

"I'm really surprised you came tonight, Toddy," Mrs. Blanchard said. "I heard Helene was far from well."

Instantly, Toddy felt her criticism. Mrs. Blanchard believed Toddy's place was at Helene's bedside.

"Oh, she's feeling much better, Mrs. Blanchard. Mrs. Hale thinks she overdid Christmas. Helene adores the holidays and the—"

"You should be very grateful to be in such a nice household," Mrs. Blanchard cut in coldly. "Sad to say, not all you orphans were so fortunate, like that—the one who's staying with Miss Cady—what's her name?"

Toddy tried to hide her indignation. "Kit Ternan, ma'am."

"Yes, that poor thing. And did you see that awful dress she wore to graduation? Imagine living out at the Hansens all these years. *You* could have landed there. You should thank your lucky stars, Toddy."

"Why, mother?" Chris was back, all smiles and glowing happiness.

Mrs. Blanchard passed off his question with a nervous little laugh. "Oh, nothing, son. Just girl talk. Why don't you take Toddy into the parlor and introduce her to your aunts and uncles?"

"Good idea." Chris held out his hand to Toddy, who took it gratefully. "Come on, Toddy."

Toddy's insides felt flaming hot. To Mrs. Blanchard, Toddy would always be an outsider, forever one of those Orphan Train riders set apart from the rest of Meadowridge.

"Did I tell you how smashing you look tonight?" Chris whispered as they stood at the parlor doorway. Toddy looked at him with a rush of gratitude.

She was sorry Chris's mother did not approve of her, but she refused to let it spoil her evening. Who cared what Mrs. Blanchard or anyone else thought of her when someone as handsome and nice as Chris thought she hung the moon?

Before long, Toddy had met Chris's balding uncles and plump aunts. The uncles were jovial and friendly. The aunts were a different cup of tea altogether. Toddy felt like they were sizing her up, deciding whether she was "right" for their favorite nephew.

At last, everyone went into the dining room. It looked like a holiday picture. On the white linen and lace tablecloth stood two silver candlesticks with tall red candles. In the middle was a centerpiece of white carnations ringed in holly, bright with red berries.

As Chris held out her chair, Toddy sat down, determined now more than ever to show the Blanchards she matched their manners.

Mrs. Blanchard sat at one end talking with her sisters.

Mrs. Hale's words floated back into Toddy's mind. "Don't let Bernice Blanchard intimidate you. She'll try." Don't worry, Mrs. Hale, Toddy resolved silently. I won't.

As course followed delicious course—clear soup, salad, white fish, roast lamb, five vegetables, pudding, pecan pie, glazed fruit and mints—Toddy managed the entire dinner using the right silverware, even down to the ivory-handled fruit knife and finger bowls.

She was pleased and a little proud of herself. It was in this happy frame of mind that she agreed to join Chris's young cousins when they begged her to play hide-and-seek.

The gentlemen remained at the table for brandy and cigars while the ladies moved to the parlor to chat. The young folk had the rest of the house in which to play. After selecting who was "It," everyone scattered looking for a good place to hide.

Chris pointed Toddy to a huge blue china vase holding peacock feathers standing in the hallway outside the parlor door. He took the steps two at a time up to the landing to hide behind a large Japanese screen.

Toddy hurried over and slid behind the vase, gathering her skirt about her and wedging herself against the wall. Gradually the sounds of running feet and muffled giggles subsided. Toddy crouched there, waiting. It was then she heard Mrs. Blanchard's voice coming from the parlor.

"I thought his being away would cool things off."

Another voice said, "You know, Bernice, forbidden fruit tastes sweetest!"

"She's got quite a few airs for someone with no background."

Toddy's throat instantly went dry. The women were talking about *her*.

"You must admit she's a pretty little thing, for an orphan."

"That may be, Ethel, but you *must* understand how I feel."

Quietly, Toddy slipped out from behind the vase and crept up the stairs to join Chris.

He pulled her close. "Hey, this is cozy!"

"I have to go home," she said crossly, tugging her hand away.

"Home? Right now?" He was surprised. "Aren't you having a good time? We don't have to play with the kids, you know."

Toddy shook her head. "No, I mean, yes. It's not the game, Chris. It's just that—" she hesitated, unable to think of an excuse. Then she remembered. "I'd like to get home in time to tell Helene good night. She hasn't been feeling well."

Chris gave a heavy sigh. "Helene! It's always Helene, Toddy."

"Well, she is my sister and—" Toddy stopped cold.

Was she? Did Helene really consider her a sister? Or was Toddy just hoping she did? All at once, Toddy felt terribly insecure. Tears rushed into her eyes, and she turned away quickly so Chris couldn't see them.

But he knew something was wrong. He touched her arm. "I'm sorry, Toddy," he said gently. "I didn't mean to offend you. Look, if you want to go home, we'll go, right now."

Toddy forced a smile. "I'm not mad. Honest," she whispered back. "It's just that Helene never gets to go to parties, and she loves to hear about everything I do. If she's still awake when I get back, I can share everything that happened with her."

"Sure, Toddy, I understand."

Politely, Toddy told everyone good night and thanked Chris's mother. Mrs. Blanchard smiled, but her eyes were as cold as the night outside as she held the front door open for them.

"Now, Chris, hurry back. Uncle Jim wants to have a man-to-man talk with you about college. You won't keep him, will you, Toddy? And do wish Mrs. Hale a happy New Year for me, won't you?"

As they went down the steps and out the gate, Chris took one of Toddy's hands and put it with his into the deep pocket of his coat. The touch of his palm against hers was comforting, but Toddy's heart still stung painfully from the cruel words she had overheard.

"What a night," Chris said, looking up at the sky where hundreds of sparkling stars sprinkled the vast dark canopy above. He squeezed Toddy's hand. "I'm glad you wanted to leave early. We'll get to say happy New Year to each other alone."

Toddy didn't answer. Her throat felt sore. The cutting discussion about her had hurt. No matter how she tried to dismiss it, it felt like a hangnail or a stone bruise in her heart.

To Chris's mother, she would always be an Orphan Train waif. Living with Helene and Mrs. Hale, loving Chris or even his loving her made no difference. Maybe it never would.

"Toddy—" Chris stopped under a lamppost and put his hands on her shoulders. He slowly turned her around to the light so he could see her face. "Mother was right about Uncle Jim wanting to talk to me. But it's not about college." Chris's voice showed some excitement.

"I talked with him earlier today. He has a construction firm in Brookhaven, only fifty miles from here. You know I've always liked working with my hands and being out of doors. I hate the thought of working in a bank like my father. That's my mother's idea."

He hesitated. "So, what do you think? If he'll let me go to work for him, I'll quit college after this semester and then—and then, Toddy, I could support a wife. I mean, Toddy, you know how much I love you. There's never been anyone else but you. Will you marry me?"

Stunned, Toddy stared up at Chris. "But, Chris, your parents will never agree to that!"

His handsome face grew stubborn.

"I don't want to go back to the university. I don't want to wait three more years." His hands gripped her shoulders tightly. "I'm afraid something will happen. I'm afraid I'll lose you."

Toddy knew Chris loved her. She saw it in his eyes, heard it in his voice, and felt it in his touch. She had missed him more than she thought possible the past three months while he had been away. And these last two weeks he'd been home for the holidays had been heaven.

For a moment she allowed herself to believe a wonderful fairy tale was coming true. She and Chris, childhood friends, high school sweethearts, destined for happiness. A home of their own, something Toddy had always longed for. Someone to love her and someone she could love.

"What do you say, Toddy? Will you? You do love me, don't you?"

The chill of the night air reached inside Toddy's coat and made her shiver. Chris quickly put his arm around her and drew her close.

"You don't need to answer that. I know you do. And we'll work it out. Come on, you're getting cold. I'll get you home. Then tonight, I'll talk to Uncle Jim. I'll get him to convince my folks this is really what I want to do."

The temperature had dropped, and the sidewalks were now crusted over with a thin layer of ice. The air was so cold it was almost hard to draw a deep breath. As the couple rounded the corner and started up the hill toward

117

the Hales' house, Toddy stopped short. She clutched Chris's arm.

"Oh, Chris, look!" she gasped. "That's Dr. Woodward's buggy in front of the house! Helene must be worse!"

Before finishing the sentence, Toddy broke away and started to run.

A red-eyed Clara Hubbard met her at the bottom of the curved staircase.

"Oh, Toddy!"

"Clara, what happened?"

Clara pulled a handkerchief out of her apron pocket and blew her nose.

"Miss Helene had a heart seizure, Toddy. Dr. Woodward was here because we'd called him earlier when Miss Helene started having trouble breathing." She held the crumpled handkerchief to her mouth. "Thank goodness the doctor was here!"

A short while later after Chris had left, Toddy huddled on the top step of the stairway, a few feet from Helene's bedroom door. Locked in misery, she crossed her arms, hugging herself as she rocked back and forth.

"Oh, please, dear God, help Helene get well," Toddy prayed desperately.

Her teeth began to chatter, and she had to clench them to stop. Deep shuddering waves of panic swept over her. Abandoned again! The strong feelings clutched at her throat like a viper. She couldn't lose Helene. Helene was the only one who loved her just as she was— unconditionally.

Toddy knew it wasn't right to bargain with God, but tonight she didn't know what else to do. "Just let her get well," she pleaded. "I'll read the Bible more like Helene wants me to. I won't be in any more plays. I'll devote my whole life to helping people. Just please let her get well!"

No matter what anyone else thought, Helene was her sister. Of all the people in her life, Toddy knew Helene was the only one who loved her just as she was. If she lost Helene, the world would be empty.

Then, from a dark cavern deep within her soul came that same jeering voice she heard so often: "You're nothin' but a scrawny theater brat. If anything happens to Miss Helene . . ."

Toddy shrank back. What would happen to her if Helene—Toddy hugged her arms about herself. She couldn't think about it. Nothing was going to happen to Helene. Nothing *could* happen to Helene.

Just then Helene's door opened, and Dr. Woodward stepped out into the hall. Mrs. Hale followed him. Toddy quickly scrambled up and stepped back into the shadows.

"Well, she's passed this crisis," the doctor said. "She'll probably sleep for a few hours. But she's not to be left alone. Someone should be at her bedside in case she has trouble breathing again."

The two of them headed toward the staircase.

"How serious was this?" Mrs. Hale asked.

"Olivia, in Helene's state, anything can be serious."

"I wish we could have gotten away sooner," fretted Mrs. Hale. "You know I was planning to take the girls to Europe in March, Doctor. Should I wait until spring?"

During the long pause, Toddy found herself holding her breath.

"My dear Mrs. Hale, I don't think when you go makes a great deal of difference."

The doctor stopped at the banister and faced her. "What I'm trying to say, Olivia, is that it doesn't matter whether Helene goes to Europe or stays in Meadowridge. She's only twenty-three, but she has the heart of a person three times her age, and it's wearing out." The doctor heaved a heavy sigh. "Helene may have only a year or less to live."

Toddy was not sure whether it was Mrs. Hale's moan or her own she heard. A year! One year, twelve months. Helene had only a year to live!

Gone were all the fantasies of running away with Chris and living a dream. Gone was the thought of sharing her life with him. Gone was her wonderful life as Helene's sister.

Toddy's knees felt like Clara's rice pudding. She slid down the wall and crumpled into a pile on the rug, choking back the sobs within her.

Then Toddy stopped and swallowed hard. No, she told herself sternly, she had faced hard times before. She could do this. She *must* do this. It was time now to put away childish fantasies. Helene needed her. If they had only a year, Toddy would make sure it was the happiest year Helene had ever known.

Germany

The German hotel dining room was elegant, with gold-framed mirrors, white linen tablecloths on round tables, thick carpeting, and deep rich drapes. Just outside the big picture windows, the terrace was covered by a recent November snow. Beyond it lay the beautiful German Alps.

A tall waiter with the military bearing of a Prussian officer approached their table and in heavily accented English asked, "Vill der be anysing else, Modam?"

"I think not," Mrs. Hale replied, signing the check he presented on a small silver tray.

Olivia sat back to finish the remainder of her after-dinner coffee.

Toddy and Helene sat opposite her. "Look at that lady over there," she heard Toddy whisper to Helene. "She looks like a princess. I imagine her father is a Bavarian prince."

"Oh, yes!" Helene supplied. "And one time he was traveling along the Rhine River when all of a sudden . . ."

The two girls were playing one of their favorite games—imagining the life stories of their fellow diners. Olivia was glad they enjoyed it so much. There certainly had not been much for them to do during their stay here, especially for Toddy. Most of the guests at the luxurious hotel were middle-aged people who neither spoke nor understood English. Not that Toddy ever complained. She seemed completely devoted to Helene, accompanying her to her doctor's appointments and spending hours in the waiting rooms. Then afterward when Helene was tired, Toddy would read aloud to her until she fell asleep. No real sisters could have been closer.

Olivia folded her napkin and placed it beside the empty cup and saucer. She was having a hard time entering into their joy. Her desperate search for a cure for Helene's condition had led her nowhere. Even the German specialist they had just seen had supported Dr. Woodward. All the traveling and clinics and possibilities of treatments had twisted her trail right back to the same diagnosis: Helene's heart was giving out.

Just then a burst of laughter floated across the table. Helene buried her mouth in her napkin while Toddy reached for a glass of water. Olivia blinked back the tears brimming in her own eyes as she observed the two girls. Toddy's face glowed with a healthy sheen from their weeks in Switzerland, while Helene looked frailer and paler, her dark eyes larger than her thin face.

Resentment stabbed Olivia's heart. Why Helene? What good was all Olivia's money if it couldn't buy the one thing she wanted—her granddaughter's health?

Suddenly Olivia felt weary. She was tired of traveling and tired of foreign countries and people speaking languages she could not understand. She was tired of looking at her phrase book so she could translate ordinary words. She longed for the simple life of Meadowridge, to be in her own comfortable house, eating foods without strange names, and sleeping in her own bed.

Olivia wanted to go home.

"I'll go say good night to Grandmother, then I'll be in," Helene later told Toddy when they got off the elevator at their suite.

Toddy was sitting up in bed braiding her hair when Helene came in about a half-hour later. Helene sat at the foot of the bed and watched Toddy for a few minutes before speaking.

"Anything the matter?" Toddy asked.

"I think Grandmother wants to go home, Toddy."

"To Meadowridge? But I thought she wanted to go back to Paris."

"She did, at first, but now she says she's anxious to get back to the States, to get settled in her own home again. I think she feels we've been gone long enough." Helene's big dark eyes were troubled.

"The real reason, I think, is what she's not saying, Toddy. She's discouraged. The European doctors she was told so much about can't fix my heart. But then, Dr. Woodward told her not to put her hopes in them."

Something cold clutched Toddy's own heart. She hoped Helene had not overheard Mrs. Hale and Dr. Woodward that night in the hallway.

"So, will we be leaving soon?"

"That's what we were talking about. I told her I wanted to discuss it with you." Helene scooted in closer, and Toddy put down her brush.

"You see, Toddy, I have an idea. I've always wanted to spend Christmas in Austria, and we're so close!" She took a deep breath. "What would you think of letting Grandmother go ahead to London and arrange for our passage home while you and I stay another few weeks and celebrate Christmas in Austria?"

"Helene, what do you think your grandmother will say to that?"

"I'm sure she'll agree, especially if we go to Badgastein, the well-known health resort." Helene smiled, "It's not as though we were children anymore. You're twenty and I'm almost twenty-five. And after all, it is almost 1902! We're living in the twentieth century, not the dark ages."

After much discussion, Mrs. Hale gave in to the girls' request. After seeing the girls off on the train to Salzburg, Olivia left Munich for London, where she would make arrangements for their journey home.

Upon their arrival in the Alpine valley of Badgastein, the girls took a horse-drawn sleigh sent by the hotel to take them up the snowy hill to the rambling, rustic chalet. Along the way, they saw winding streets thronged with tourists and townspeople dressed in traditional costumes. They saw men in vests, wool shorts, and ribboned knee socks. The women wore swinging flowered skirts. The shop windows were bright with all sorts of gifts, and the streets were gaily decorated for the season. Through the clear, crystal air rang the sound of music provided by a colorful band.

"It looks exactly like one of the toy villages people set up under their Christmas trees, doesn't it?" exclaimed Helene, squeezing Toddy's arm under the wool blanket draped around them.

Perched on a cliff, the hotel looked like a picture in a fairy-tale book. In the lobby, comfortable chairs were arranged around a fire, blazing in a wide stone fireplace. Everyone was friendly and smiling, a welcome change from the hotel in Munich.

Toddy and Helene followed the bellhop up a broad staircase to their two rooms. Each opened onto its own little balcony. The furnishings were simple. Helene immediately sank into the large bed with its white quilt and piles of feather pillows.

"This will be wonderful!" Helene exclaimed, looking happier than Toddy had seen her in weeks.

As Toddy unpacked some of Helene's things and placed them in the hand-painted dresser, a dart of hope sprang up in her. Maybe this was exactly what Helene needed.

Their stay took on its own enjoyable routine. Helene's mornings were taken up with a treatment in the spa followed by an hour's rest. Then she met Toddy for lunch. Sometimes when the sun was bright, they were even able to eat in the hotel's outdoor restaurant, surrounded by snow-covered hills glistening like gems. They spent their afternoons strolling along the snow-packed walks, exploring the small gift shops, or having pastries in one of the small cafés in town.

"It's all so magical!" Toddy declared.

"It's a long way from Meadowridge, isn't it?" laughed Helene as she stirred the whipped cream swirling around the top of her café mocha.

At that moment Toddy noticed a passing group of young men dressed in traditional costumes just outside the café. One of them reminded her of Chris. For a brief moment, she felt a sharp twinge of regret. She had not spoken with him since the day she had told him she could not marry him. It was all for the best. There was no room in her life now for romance.

Two days before Christmas Eve they watched the annual Christmas parade through the middle of town. It ended with the arrival of St. Nicholas, the Austrian name for Santa Claus. People lined the streets to cheer him and shout as he passed by, calling back the greeting *"Froehliche weinachten,"* which means joyful Christmas. The children squealed as the jolly "saint" passed out delicious chocolate candies.

125

When they arrived back at the chalet, Helene squeezed Toddy's arm. "Oh, look," she said, "how beautiful!"

At the center of the lobby stood a Christmas tree decorated with angels, birds, flowers, and painted balls. Draped with garland and silver tinsel, the tree gleamed with dozens of tiny candles. A single star at the top nearly touched the vaulted ceiling.

"Isn't it perfect?" Helene sighed happily.

When the girls got to their rooms, Toddy insisted they order room service to bring up supper so Helene could rest. She looked pale and drained after the parade.

"Remember, there's a party for the hotel guests tomorrow," Toddy said as she dumped her packages on her bed. "You don't want to be tired and miss it."

But Helene did miss it. Too weak to get up the next morning, she sent down word to the hotel doctor. He dropped by later to check her condition.

"It's my fault, Helene," Toddy told her as she stood by her bedside. "I've let us crowd too much into these days before Christmas. From now on we'll slow down our pace."

Although her face was pale and drained, Helene smiled. "It's not your fault, Toddy. I just overdid it a bit. I'll be fine after I've rested a while."

On Christmas Eve, the two young ladies bundled up and went out on the balcony to watch the townspeople in the folk costumes walk by on their way to Midnight Mass. The sound of clanging church bells rang across the snow. And to Helene's joy, the people were singing her favorite Christmas carol, "Silent Night."

"Oh, Toddy, this has to be my happiest Christmas ever," she sighed.

On Christmas morning, the maid brought Toddy her usual breakfast. As she was eating, she discovered a note from the hotel doctor, asking her to come to his office.

Toddy quickly dressed, peeked into Helene's room to see if she was still asleep, and went straight downstairs.

"Your sister's condition is getting worse," he told her gravely. "The treatments we have here cannot stop the progress of her disease."

A tidal wave of fear washed over every ounce of her. Toddy held onto the arm of the chair in which she was sitting as if it would stop the storm from overtaking her.

"Miss Hale is living on borrowed time. Every day is a miracle."

Toddy swallowed hard. "What do you suggest we do?"

The doctor stroked his trimmed beard for a moment. "I cannot advise travel. It would be too dangerous. I think you should notify Miss Hale's grandmother—"

Toddy left the doctor's office in a trance. Instead of returning to her room, she went outside and blindly turned onto one of the trails that wound through the snow-covered woods. She turned on Empress Elizabeth Walk. It had been named after the mother of a prince who had mysteriously died. It was said that the heartbroken mother often walked along this trail mourning her only son.

Toddy's heart was breaking too. The anxiety she had held back all these months fell on her like a lead weight. She now realized that all the hopeful signs she had looked for were only her own wishful thinking. The sparkling snow around her dimmed as tears blinded her eyes.

Helene's time was nearly up, her days numbered. The fear the Hale household had lived with all these years was about to come upon them.

Why? Oh, why must Helene be taken away from her? Bitter sobs rushed up in Toddy's throat, and she stopped. Leaning her arm against a tree, she put her head on it and wept.

At length, she straightened up. The tears had not eased the pain, but they had strengthened her spirit. She wiped her eyes with her mittens and blew her nose. If I can act in a play, then I can act now. If this is the only time we have, I'll make it the best time of all, she resolved. Turning around, she walked slowly back to the hotel.

Because Helene was still asleep when she returned, Toddy had a chance to wash her face and pull herself together. By the time Helene was up, Toddy was her old merry self.

But the two girls had been together too long for Helene not to notice Toddy's mood.

"Toddy, dear, don't be sad," Helene said as she reached out and covered Toddy's hand with her thin hand. "I know, and it's all right. I've known for a long time."

"But you must get well, Helene!" Tears now streamed down Toddy's cheeks.

Helene patted her hand. "I'm not in any pain or even unhappy about it anymore, Toddy. It's really all right."

"But we'll go somewhere, find another doctor. I won't accept it! I *can't* accept it! I'll keep praying—"

Helene laid back on the fluffy pillows. "Let's enjoy what we have. Now, this day, this minute."

Toddy slipped off the bed, knelt beside Helene, holding onto her hand.

"I can't lose you, Helene," she sobbed. "There must be something we can do!"

Helene smoothed back Toddy's curls. "Toddy, would it help to know you have made all the difference in my life? Dear little sister, without you my life would've been so lonely."

Helene began to cry also, and for a while the two girls clung to each other helplessly. Then they talked, sharing all the deep things in their hearts, agreeing to make the best of the time they had together.

The next morning Helene was too weak to get up. Toddy refused to leave her, and that afternoon as she sat by her bedside, Helene slipped quietly away. Toddy was still holding her hand. It was December 26, 1901.

A short while later, Toddy walked outside into the fading daylight. Numbed by her grief, she headed through the village to cross a little arched bridge at the end of the street. There she found herself in the churchyard of a small chapel. She pushed open the heavy wood doors and walked inside. Only a flickering lamp near the altar lighted the interior.

There was a quietness here that somehow gave Toddy comfort. She advanced up the short aisle to the wooden kneelers in front of the small altar and knelt down. Peace wrapped itself around her like a warm cloak.

All the questions she had about Helene's death needed answers. The only thing that came into her mind was a Scripture verse she had learned long ago in Sunday school: "Be still, and know that I am God."

Toddy did not know how long she knelt there. As she got to her feet and started out of the chapel, she saw a wall plaque lettered in beautiful German script: *Auf Wiedersehen*. In English, she knew this meant, "Farewell. Good-bye. Until we meet again."

As Toddy pushed open the chapel door, she looked back at the altar.

"*Auf Wiedersehen,* dear Helene," she whispered.

18

Olivia could not act or think as she normally did, so Toddy took charge of making the arrangements for Helene's body to go with them on the long, sad journey home. The gray drab London winter weather did nothing to lift their grief. It wasn't long before Toddy realized that her presence reminded Mrs. Hale of Helene, so she began to keep to herself.

The earliest possible sailing date was three weeks after Toddy's arrival in London. During the long days, Toddy had much time to think about her past and look at the future. She would leave her room in the Claridge Hotel early in the morning and take long walks along the strange city streets, under skies gray with fog. Her heart was heavy and her thoughts troubled.

"If anything happens to Helene—" The words taunted her. Now something *had* happened to Helene. What would become of Toddy?

With all her faith, Toddy knew Helene was at peace now. But the old wound of abandonment wouldn't let her grief at the loss go away. Nothing could fill the void in her life. The whole world seemed empty now that that one dear face was missing.

When at last they boarded the ship for the voyage home, Mrs. Hale retired to her cabin and remained there most of the time. Toddy walked the decks or sat bundled in a deck chair looking out at the sea. The open book in her lap would often lay unread as she stared into space, asking herself, what now?

She must do something with her life. But what? Once back in Meadowridge, Mrs. Hale would not need her. Her thoughts turned to Kit and Laurel. With dismay, she realized she really did not have any long-term goals like her two friends. Kit had always wanted to write, and Laurel had always been able to sing. What gifts did she have? She thought about Pastor Scott's sermon about Moses. What special rod had God given her? Why couldn't she see it? Now, with Helene gone, Toddy wanted *her* life to count for something.

Two days out of New York, Toddy paced the deck deep in thought. The sea air sprinkled her wavy hair with its salty spray. She pulled the fur collar of her brown wool coat closer to her.

Oh, Helene, she thought, I need your help. What should I do?

Toddy looked over the rail. She could just hear Helene telling her it would all work out. "Just pray about it, dear," Helene would have said.

Of course, that's what she should have been doing all along. But Toddy hadn't been able to pray since Helene's death. She would begin and then her thoughts would drift as she remembered snatches of their conversations and experiences together. What began as prayer ended as painful memories.

But today, as the wind tugged at her hat and veil, the words of a psalm floated into her mind. "Show me thy ways, O Lord; teach me thy paths."

And Toddy prayed. "You know me, Lord. You know my heart. Lead me in the direction you would have me go in my life."

On the night before they were to dock, Mrs. Hale called Toddy into her stateroom.

"Toddy, there are some things we need to talk about." The deep lines of grief in Mrs. Hale's face gave way as she talked. "I've been thinking about a memorial service for Helene when we get back to Meadowridge. I'd like you to choose something to say on her tombstone. You were closer to her than anyone, Toddy. You'll know what she would like best."

"Yes, I'll think about it," Toddy promised.

"There's something else." Mrs. Hale picked up an envelope from the bureau and handed it to Toddy. "Now that Helene is gone, you must begin to think of your own future. You know how much Helene loved you, Toddy. What you don't know is that she was independently wealthy. She inherited a great deal of money from her father, my son."

Olivia pressed her lips together to hold back her emotions. So many losses. So much tragedy. Somehow, she would walk though this too, but she didn't know how.

"Let's sit down." Mrs. Hale motioned her to the sofa.

Toddy sat down still holding the unopened envelope in her hands.

"When you graduated from high school, Helene had a long talk with me, Toddy," Mrs. Hale began. "She always knew her life hung by a thread, and she insisted on making out a will before we left for Europe.

"What you have in your hand, Toddy, is a copy of her will. She made you her chief beneficiary."

Toddy raised her eyebrows in an unspoken question.

"That means she left you most of her estate. She wanted you to be free and independent like she was. The difference is that you have the health to travel and accomplish your goals." An expression of sadness passed briefly over Mrs. Hale's face, then she continued. "Until you are twenty-one, my signature will be required on any withdrawals you make. I am the guardian of the trust fund Helene set up."

Toddy opened her mouth to say something, but she couldn't think of what to say.

"If you want to go to college and pursue a career or even return to Europe, the funds are there."

Up until that moment, Toddy's mind had not been made up. All of a sudden, everything became clear. It was true that she loved drama and acting. But she loved people even more. It had been Helene's book about Florence Nightingale that had gripped her heart. Toddy had helped Helene; she wanted to help others too. This would be her gift—back to Helene.

"Mrs. Hale, I think I know," she said quietly. "I believe I would like to be a nurse."

Mrs. Hale's eyes twinkled for the first time in weeks. She smiled. "A splendid idea, Toddy. You'll make a fine nurse. Helene would be very proud of you."

19

Good Samaritan Hospital, St. Louis

The rising bell shrilled down the hall, echoing into every room in the dormitory.

Toddy moaned and pulled the blanket up over her head. Only a faint gray light seeped in through the high windows. The winter morning was still dark. She squeezed her eyes shut more tightly. Could she possibly sneak ten more minutes of sleep?

All around her Toddy heard familiar sounds: groans, creaking bedsprings, opening drawers, and swishing water being poured into washbowls. Five thirty! Only twenty minutes to get up, put on her pink muslin uniform, button her starched white pinafore, pull on her black cotton stockings, and lace up her black shoes. Then over to the chapel for morning prayers. After that it was the hospital dining room for a fast breakfast of oatmeal and coffee. Ward duty at the Nurses' Training School of Good Samaritan Hospital in St. Louis started at seven sharp.

For the next twelve hours, the nursing student would not have a minute to call her own. First, she would sweep and mop the ward floor, then scrub every unoccupied bed and change the sheets. While the third-year students bathed the patients, new students like Toddy set up breakfast trays, fetched coal, and filled water pitchers. Classes were held from ten until three with a half hour break for lunch. After distributing dinner trays to patients at five, Toddy helped get them ready for bed, only to return to her dorm to study. At ten, when the "lights out" bell rang, Toddy usually could barely hold her eyes open.

She had never imagined how hard it would be. Most of her classmates were hearty farm girls from the Midwest, used to hard chores at home. But what Toddy lacked in physical strength, she made up for in energy and a fierce determination to succeed. Toddy made it through the first six-month period and finally traded her pink uniform for a blue-striped one.

One afternoon Toddy was taking a quick break in her dormitory room when she was told she had a visitor. Puzzled, she got up from her cot, straightened her white apron, and went downstairs.

"Hello, Toddy." The voice was familiar.

Toddy blinked her eyes. To her surprise, Bernice Blanchard sat primly in one of the parlor chairs.

"Mrs. Blanchard!" Toddy almost gasped. "How, ah, nice to see you."

"Well, Toddy, you look well." The woman's steel eyes were taking in every inch. "I guess you're wondering why I'm here." She paused and pursed her mouth. "Mr. Blanchard is attending a banking conference here in St. Louis, and I came with him. Mrs. Hale told me you were here, so I thought I'd just come over and pay you a little visit. This way I can give Olivia a report on how you're getting along."

"Oh, I'm just fine," she quickly replied. The woman's eyes narrowed, and Toddy wondered what her true motive was.

"I'm very glad to see you're doing something useful with your life, Toddy. One cannot expect handouts forever. I'm sure it's a great burden off Olivia to have you on your own."

By now, Toddy's hands were clenched inside her apron pocket. She stood as stiff as her high starched collar.

"I do hope you'll take this in the spirit intended, Toddy." Mrs. Blanchard shifted her fur neck piece before continuing. "But I feel you ought to know that Chris is back from South America. Poor dear, he looked dreadful when he returned home, so thin and sallow. Anyway, he has decided to go back to the university to get his engineering degree."

Toddy hadn't moved from the doorway.

"Of course, you know he ran off to those awful jungles after you left. But I want you to understand that his father and I feel like he's finally on the right track. And I'm hoping you won't try to contact him or pick up any old threads of your relationship with him."

Mrs. Blanchard twisted the chain of her beaded handbag as she talked. "What's past is past. Our son has a fine future ahead of him and—"

Toddy could not stand it a minute longer.

"Mrs. Blanchard, I understand you completely." Her tone was cold. "Let me set your mind at ease. I have no intention of contacting Chris. And as for my interfering—"

"Well, I wouldn't put it so bluntly," stammered Mrs. Blanchard.

"You've made yourself quite clear." Toddy checked her watch, the same watch the Hales had given her for graduation. "And now, if you'll excuse me, I go on duty in ten minutes." Toddy extended her arm toward the dormitory door. "Good-bye, Mrs. Blanchard. You may tell Mr. Blanchard you accomplished your mission."

Toddy turned and with all the dignity she could muster, left the parlor and started up the stairs.

Now more than ever, Toddy understood fully what she had always known. The Blanchards did not approve of her for their son. They had never accepted her. And any hope Toddy might have entertained about a future with Chris had to be put away forever.

20

Because she was naturally outgoing and friendly, Toddy was at her best with the patients. When she gave them a bath, brought food trays, or delivered medication, she always managed a cheery greeting and listening ear.

This was especially true with one patient, Mrs. Agnes O'Malley, an elderly woman who had been admitted for surgery. Because she was tiny and frail, the doctors wanted her to gain some weight and strength before her operation. During the time Toddy cared for her, the two formed a special relationship.

"Well, I am worried about one thing," Mrs. O'Malley confided in her strong Irish accent. "My animals. I have a canary and two cats. You know, dear, they're such creatures of habit."

While Toddy had never owned an animal, she understood. She nodded as she gently smoothed the sheets and fluffed up the pillow behind the patient's head.

"And pretty soon, my rosebushes will need pruning..."

From chatting with Mrs. O'Malley every day, Toddy got a mental picture of her small cozy house, her two cats, and the bright yellow canary in its cage in the window of her snug little kitchen.

On the day of the surgery, Toddy prepared the patient and held her hand as they wheeled her down the corridor to the operating room.

"I'll be here when you wake up, Mrs. O'Malley," Toddy promised.

But Mrs. O'Malley never woke up. Toddy hid in a linen closet and wept when she found out. While she knew she should not have become emotionally involved with a patient, Toddy had wanted to help. Like herself, Mrs. O'Malley had been alone in the world. As the young nurse cried, her old feelings of abandonment flowed out like a rushing river. She buried her head in her hands. All her hard work to become a nurse, the long hours of study, the tiredness. Did any of it matter? Was helping others really her gift? Was this where she belonged?

When Toddy returned to her dorm room late that evening, she spotted Helene's Bible on the bedstand. She had brought it with her. Oh, how she missed Helene's soft voice reading aloud. She picked up the worn book, flipped it open, and began to read.

"For my thoughts are not your thoughts, neither are your ways my ways, saith the Lord."

While Toddy believed this Scripture in Isaiah, she couldn't feel it right now. She felt all alone. Sleep would not come easily tonight.

At the end of the school year, Toddy returned to Meadowridge. As she boarded the train in the St. Louis station, her mind was making another trip. Had it been nearly thirteen years since she had journeyed out West on the Orphan Train? Peering out of the open railroad car window, Toddy remembered how bleak her days at Greystone would have been without Laurel and Kit. A smile crossed her lips just as the whistle gave a shrill toot. Yes, they would always be friends. In spite of the fact Kit was now in San Francisco and Laurel lived in Boston, their promise to be friends held them together like glue. They were truly "Three Musketeers."

When the car suddenly lurched forward, Toddy's thoughts shifted to Hale House and Helene. Her beloved Helene. Toddy was returning to Meadowridge to help Mrs. Hale dedicate an addition to the Meadowridge Library—a children's room. Helene had left money in her will for the project.

As the steam engine picked up speed, Toddy felt some misgivings. It had been over a year since she had been in Meadowridge. What would it be like after all this time? What would the Hale house be like now, without Helene?

"Meadowridge! Next stop, Meadowridge!"

The conductor's words abruptly jolted Toddy back to the present. Since she had not sent word of the exact time of her arrival, she did not expect anyone to meet her at the busy train station. Leaving her suitcase to be delivered later, she began walking along the familiar streets from the depot toward the Hale house.

At the gate of the Victorian mansion, she paused, imagining Helene's face at one of the upstairs windows. For a moment, Toddy stood there with her hand on the iron latch before slowly slipping it up and pushing the gate open.

The door opened as Mrs. Hale, tall, elegant, her hair grayer than Toddy remembered, stepped out on the porch.

With longing in her heart, Toddy halted. Then Olivia held out both of her arms. At that, Toddy dropped her valise and ran up the steps into her embrace. The two hugged one another for a long time.

"Welcome home, my dear!" Olivia whispered. "How I've missed you."

Toddy leaned her head on Olivia's shoulder and sobbed. She was wanted. She belonged. For the first time in her life, she felt like she had come home at last.

The day of the dedication was very warm. The noon ceremony took place in the main library at the doorway into the children's room. Many prominent people from Meadowridge attended, including the mayor. Following the ceremony, a ladies' group had set up a reception out on the side lawn.

Mrs. Hale and Toddy stood in the receiving line, shaking hands with everyone who wanted to express thanks. Looking down the line, Toddy noticed a woman with a large hat trimmed with blue flowers. To her dismay it was Bernice Blanchard. Everything inside Toddy wanted to run away.

As Mrs. Blanchard approached, a strange thing happened however.

"Have you met my *other* granddaughter?" Mrs. Hale was introducing Toddy to the couple right in front of her. Her voice was quite clear, and Mrs. Blanchard, next in line, could not have failed to hear.

"How nice to meet you, dear. I know you are so proud of your sister," the lady said politely as she shook Toddy's hand.

Mrs. Blanchard was next in line. She held out a limp hand. "A lovely occasion, Olivia," she mumbled.

Toddy felt some satisfaction that Bernice Blanchard seemed to be at a loss for words. Then at that moment, the woman's round face suddenly turned beet red. Her eyes rolled back, and her knees buckled until she fell onto the grass.

Without a second thought, Toddy sprang into action. "Get back, everyone, give her air!" she commanded.

Toddy knelt down and loosened the buttons on the side of Mrs. Blanchard's high lace collar. She slipped one arm under her shoulders, raised the woman slightly, and with her other free hand, removed the hat.

"Someone soak some napkins with ice water and bring them to me," Toddy ordered.

By now, Mrs. Blanchard's hair had come out of its pins and was falling over her face. Toddy unhooked the tight sash around her plump waist. When the wet napkins arrived, she pressed one against the patient's neck and another against her forehead.

Soon, a low moan escaped from Mrs. Blanchard's pale lips and her eyelids began to flutter. At the same time, Mr. Blanchard pushed through the wide ring of gawkers, wiping his bald head.

"It's all right, dearie," he said as he squatted down beside her. "I'm here now. We'll get you home. You're going to be fine." He looked up at Toddy.

"I'll come with you," Toddy said.

About that time, the crowd made a path for Dr. Woodward.

"Good work." He nodded to Toddy.

"I'll get the carriage," Mr. Blanchard said.

For the first time since Toddy could remember, Mrs. Blanchard stayed quiet. By the time her husband had returned, the doctor had made his diagnosis. The sun and excitement had been too much for her.

At the Blanchard's house, Toddy helped the maid get Bernice into her nightgown and into bed.

Before she closed her eyes, Bernice reached out and took Toddy's hand.

"Thank you, Toddy," she whispered with a raspy voice. "Thank you for saving my life."

Toddy knew it had been only a slight sunstroke, but she smiled. Whatever Mrs. Blanchard believed, the real miracle was that she accepted Toddy now. God certainly *did* move in mysterious ways. Today's incident had changed things.

21

Her three years of nursing school passed quickly. One week after the state examinations, Toddy was among the first scrambling down the steps into the front hall to search the list on the bulletin board for her name. She did not have to look long or far. Zephronia Victorine Todd was at the top of the graduating class.

Graduation date was set and invitations sent out. Mrs. Hale immediately wrote back to Toddy telling her she would be there. Toddy made reservations for her in one of the nicest hotels in St. Louis.

Many of her fellow nurses had applied to hospitals near their hometowns, but Toddy had not thought much further than graduation day. So she was surprised when an offer came to apply for a position at Good Samaritan. Toddy felt unsure.

She walked into the chapel and sat there quietly. Late afternoon sunlight streamed through the stained-glass window over the altar. A picture of the Good Samaritan tending the wounds of the injured traveler looked down at her.

"Lord, I believe you've led me here. But what do I do now? Where can I serve you best? Please show me."

As she came out of the chapel, two of her friends were coming in.

One whispered, "You've got company waiting for you in the parlor, Toddy."

Maybe Mrs. Hale had come a day or so early. She hurried to see.

To her surprise, a tall young man rose to his feet as she walked in.

"Chris!" Toddy gasped.

"Hello, Toddy."

It had been over four years. The lean athletic boy she remembered had become a broad-shouldered man with strong features. He was holding a bouquet of pink and white carnations.

"Oh, Chris, how wonderful to see you!" she exclaimed. "How did you know I was here?"

Chris handed her the sweet-smelling bouquet. "My mother," he grinned with teeth as white and straight as they'd always been. "When I got home this past fall, she told me how you saved her life."

Toddy's dimples deepened as she smiled. "I didn't really, you know. But I'm so glad to see you. Please sit down." She gestured to a chair. "There's so much to catch up on."

Toddy was struck with how handsome Chris still looked. His tawny hair and tanned features hadn't changed very much. But when she saw that lopsided grin, all she could think of was how much she had missed him.

"Well, I got my degree from the university and heard from Mrs. Hale that you're graduating, at the top of your class. Congratulations, Toddy. I'm proud of you."

He hesitated. "Toddy, may I come to your graduation?"

Toddy felt her heart turn over. "Of course, you may! Chris, I can hardly believe you're really here!"

"I wasn't sure you'd see me. I didn't even hear about Helene until—" He paused for a moment. "I'm so sorry, Toddy. I know how much she meant to you."

"Thanks, Chris," Toddy replied. "Actually, that's why I'm in nursing. I want to spend my life helping other people like Helene. It's a much better profession than vaudeville." She made a comic face and rolled her eyes.

Chris reached over and took her hand.

"That sounds like the Toddy I know, generous and kind. It sounds like the Toddy I love."

Toddy drew in her breath.

"I do love you, Toddy, you know that, don't you? I always have and I always will. The main reason I came up here to see you now is that I wanted to tell you that. I haven't changed about that, Toddy. I never will. There's never been anyone else for me but you."

"Oh, Chris, don't say any more. Not now."

"Then when, Toddy?" Chris's eyes had the same boyish quality they'd always had.

"I have tomorrow to think about."

"After tomorrow?"

Toddy got to her feet, still holding the bouquet. "Chris, I have to go. There's a graduation rehearsal in twenty minutes."

"All right, Toddy. I can wait. I've waited this long." His lips curved into a smile. "I'll see you tomorrow then."

The organ music filled the hospital as the twenty nursing students marched in and took their places in the two front pews. Olivia wiped her eyes. The slim figure in white with an organdy cap perched on her shining red-gold hair made her so proud.

The loss of Helene had taken a lot out of Olivia. The stately woman fingered her gold wedding band from Ed. Time had not really erased the pain of losing her husband and son. It wasn't taking away the effect of Helene's death either. As she watched Toddy receive her certificate and RN pin, she missed Helene terribly. But over

147

the last few years, she had realized her own need. Helene's death could only rob her of Toddy if she let it, and she had become determined not to let it. Toddy was becoming a granddaughter in Olivia's heart.

And now it was time for Toddy to move on with her life. Olivia knew Chris had arrived the day before. While she had once been uncertain about this relationship, she was certain now. The love bond between these two young people had been forged years ago that day on the elementary school playground. It had remained strong in spite of time and trials. It was a union that was meant to be.

At the end of the ceremony, Toddy rushed up to her. Through eyes misted with happy tears, Olivia hugged her. Then the two women searched the crowd for one more familiar face. There at the back of the chapel he waited.

Chris! Suddenly, Toddy understood too.

At Mrs. Hale's suggestion, Toddy returned to Meadowridge, where Dr. Woodward offered her a job as his office nurse three days a week. Toddy gladly accepted.

Then one day, Chris arrived at the door.

"Toddy, you'll never guess what's happened!" He was almost out of breath he was talking so fast. "I've been offered a project in Arizona. I'll be in charge of the whole thing. It's a great opportunity, and I want you to come with me."

Toddy looked down on the pleasant houses, rolling pastures of grazing cattle, and long winding river beyond the Hale's porch. Meadowridge had been a part of her life for as long as she could remember. Could she leave it? And what about Mrs. Hale? She was now in her seventies and slowing down. Her eyesight was failing, and Toddy had been so glad to get the job with Dr. Woodward so she would be close. Could she leave?

She knew she could not wait very long to give Chris her answer.

Olivia sat in her favorite armchair in front of the bay window of the parlor. Ed's gold-framed portrait still hung over the black-marble fireplace. She smoothed the silky fabric of her black skirt with her aging hands.

"My dear, you've given me so much. I could never repay you for all the happiness you have brought my life and, of course, Helene's. Now it's your time. Go with a free heart." Olivia smiled. "A fine young man loves you. Take the life he is offering and be grateful for such love. You have my blessing."

On this particular May morning in 1908, the Hale household was stirring early. At last, the day had arrived. At noon, Christopher Blanchard and Zephronia Victorine Todd would be united in marriage.

Orchards scented the air in her bedroom with rare perfume as Toddy finished packing her bags. A soft wind blew back the long curtains at her windows. How many times had she looked into the tall mirror over her dresser or snuggled down into her soft feather bed with its ruffled pillows? Even now she could still smell the scent of sweet lavender. How many times had she enjoyed her big lion's claw tub full of bubbles since that first night so long ago?

Toddy noticed her china doll with its big blue eyes. She was still propped against the pillows of the window seat in her room. Toddy had never played with it, and yet somehow that didn't matter now. Her feelings of being abandoned and lost forever had finally gone. She was an orphan no longer. Toddy had known many happy years in this room, years she would never forget. She had already known a true "happily ever after."

As Toddy folded her last blouse, she felt both calm and excited. It was going to be a beautiful wedding. She had chosen a simple cream suit and matching lace blouse to wear. Both Kit and Laurel had been able to return home to share the day with her. The only shadow was that Helene was not here too.

Just then, she heard a knock. It was Thomas with her wedding bouquet. Mr. Ferrin had picked out beautiful lilacs, pink tulips, grape hyacinths, and lily of the valley just for her. Toddy knew Helene would have loved it just as much as she did.

A few hours later, Mr. and Mrs. Chris Blanchard walked down the steps of the Meadowridge Community Church as husband and wife.

"Before we go to your mother's for the reception, there's something I want to do," Toddy told him as they left.

Hand in hand, the couple walked together up the hill to the church cemetery. Inside, Toddy quickly found what she was looking for.

HELENE ELIZABETH HALE
1879–1902
"The Redeemed of the Lamb"

Chris thoughtfully took a few steps back, leaving Toddy standing alone beside Helene's grave. He watched her kneel and place her beautiful bridal bouquet at the headstone.

Toddy touched the soft green grass with her hand. She had deeply missed Helene this day, but she could still share its beauty with her. The flowers were her wedding story to her beloved sister.

Chris came forward as Toddy stood up. He tucked her small hand into his arm, and the couple walked out through the gate into their new life together.

About the Author

I grew up in a small Southern town, in a home of storytellers and readers, where authors were admired and books were treasured and discussed. When I was nine years old, an accident confined me to bed. As my body healed, I spent hours at a time making up stories for my paper dolls to act out. That is when I began to write stories.

As a young woman, three books had an enormous impact on me: *Magnificent Obsession, The Robe,* and *Christy.* From these novels I learned that stories held the possibility of changing lives. I wanted to learn to write books with unforgettable characters who faced choices and challenges and were so real that they lingered in readers' minds long after they finished the book.

The Orphan Train West for Young Adults series is especially dear to my heart. I first heard about these orphans when I read an *American Heritage* magazine story titled "The Children's Migration." The article told of the orphan trains taking more than 250,000 abandoned children cross country to be placed in rural homes. I knew I had to write some of their stories. Toddy, Laurel, Kit, Ivy and Allison, and April and May are all special to me. I hope you will grow to love them as much as I do.

Jane Peart lives in Fortuna, California, with her husband, Ray.

The Orphan Train West for Young Adults Series

They seek love with new families . . . and turn to God to find ultimate happiness.

The Orphan Train West for Young Adults series provides a glimpse into a fascinating and little-known chapter of American history. Based on the actual history of hundreds of orphans brought by train to be adopted by families in America's heartland, this delightful series will capture your heart and imagination.

Popular author Jane Peart brings the past to life with these heartwarming novels set in the 1800s, which trace the lives of courageous young girls who are searching for fresh beginnings and loving families. As the girls search for their purpose in life, they find strength in God's unconditional love.

Follow the girls' stories as they pursue their dreams, find love, grow in their faith, and move beyond the sorrows of the past.

Look for the other books in the Orphan Train West for Young Adults series!

Shy, sensitive Laurel is placed at Boston's Greystone Orphanage when her mother enters a sanitarium. After her mother's death, Laurel is placed on the Orphan Train with Kit and Toddy, destined for the town of Meadowridge. There she is adopted by Dr. and Mrs. Woodward, who still grieve for the daughter they lost two years earlier.

Laurel brings a breath of fresh air—and much love—into the Woodwards' home. As she grows up, though, Laurel longs to discover her true identity. Her search leads her to Boston, where she uncovers secrets from her past. But will Laurel's new life come between her and the love she desires?

KIT

After her grieving, widowed father leaves Kit, her younger brother, and her baby sister at Greystone Orphanage in Boston, Kit wants desperately to bring the family back together. But the younger children are adopted and Kit is sent West on the Orphan Train. Along the way, she and her friends, Toddy and Laurel, make a pact to be "forever friends." At the end of their journey, they each go to live with different families in the town of Meadowridge.

Kit is taken by the Hansens, a farm family who wants to adopt a girl to help the weary mother of five boys. Kit rises above her dreary situation by excelling in her schoolwork. But will she ever realize her secret longings to love and be loved?

IVY & ALLISON

Ivy Austin dreams about being adopted and leaving the orphanage, but when her life takes a strange turn, she ends up on the Orphan Train. There she meets Allison, whose pretty features and charm are sure to win her a new home. Worried that she will be overlooked by potential parents and not wanting to be left behind, Ivy acts impulsively.

As Ivy and Allison grow up together in the town of Brookdale, their past as insecure orphans still hurts, even though they have loving adoptive families. Their special friendship is a comfort, but is it strong enough to withstand the truth of Ivy's secret?

JANE PEART

Ivy & Allison

Orphan Train West
SERIES

Coming soon!
Book 5 in the
Orphan Train West
for Young Adults series:
April and May